Winter Girl

Dorothy Hamilton

Illustrated by Allan Eitzen

HERALD PRESS
Scottdale, Pennsylvania
Kitchener, Ontario

Library of Congress Cataloging in Publication Data

Hamilton, Dorothy, 1906-
    Winter girl.
    SUMMARY: Two teen-age sisters deal with a jealousy
problem and learn to get along better.
    [1. Brothers and sisters — Fiction. 2. Family life —
Fiction] I. Eitzen, Allan. II. Title.
PZ7.H18136Wi   [Fic]   75-40344
ISBN 0-8361-1787-5
ISBN 0-8361-1788-3 pbk.

To Dee Dee,
another Dorothy Hamilton,
who has encouraged me.

1

DALICE CORNELL was awake for a few minutes before she opened her eyes. As she listened to the early morning sounds she wondered why they were different. Cars went up Locust Avenue, but the motors seemed muffled and she couldn't hear the tires whir and whiz on the pavement. Then she opened her eyes and blinked. The room was filled with a light that was unusually white; and she knew that snow had fallen during the night.

She yawned and rubbed one side of her neck with a fist to ease the kink which came from sleeping on a doubled pillow. She raised up on one elbow and looked over at her sister's bed. All she could see of Anitra was a fan of her dark honey hair as it fluffed out on the blue-sprigged pillowcase.

A brushing sound came from the north window. Dalice eased out of bed and tiptoed across the room. She took a deep breath and bit her lip against the impulse to call Anitra. *She won't be ready to get up for anything. And she says she hates winter. Even if the world looked as beautiful to her, as it does to me, she wouldn't admit it.*

Dalice went back to the closet for her pink corduroy robe and snugged it around her waist with the braided silk cord. She'd had the lounging garment for three years — since she was twelve — and the sleeves were two inches short. But she loved the way it looked and felt. Frequent swishings in the washing and as many flappings on the clothesline had faded the color to pale pink and textured the fabric to the softness of pussy willows.

The fragrance of frying bacon came from downstairs. *All at once I'm hungry*, she thought. But she detoured before going to the kitchen. She padded to the landing where the steps turned to the right, liking the bristly feel of the carpet on the soles of her feet. She curled up on the window seat and slid the organdy sash curtains back on the brass rod. The early morning sun shone on a frosted and whiskered world. It made many colored jewels of ice crystals. Dalice thought of the word "iridescent." She'd looked it up one day and liked the sound of the definition, "an interplay of rainbow-like colors." Such colors were highlighted on the branches and twigs of the barberry bush. *It's like a giant spray pin laced in white and studded with diamonds*, she mused.

6

Now let me think. What can I do on a day like this after I get my work chart done?" She knew what her mother had listed as her share of the Saturday work: vacuum the living room, wax the end tables and television, put clean papers on the shelves of the pan cupboard, and polish the silver in the walnut chest. Dalice liked the idea of the work charts. It helped her organize her evenings and weekends and she knew her mother would never give extra tasks. *That's another way I'm different from Anitra,* Dalice realized. *She grumbles all the time, saying no one else has to help at home, at least not every day.*

Then a question came to Dalice's mind. *Why do I keep thinking about how Anitra and I are different? I don't think I used to — at least not very often. Is there a reason? Or is this a part of what it means to grow up?*

A whiff of frying bacon lured Dalice from the windowsill. The telephone rang as she crossed the hall. "I'll get it," she called.

A girl's voice said, "Is this Anitra?"

"No. I'm her sister."

"Oh — I saw you at the drugstore with Anitra and heard her call you by name. It's Alice, isn't it?"

Whoever you are, Dalice thought, *you're new in town. No one calls me Alice anymore.* "I'll call Anitra," she said. It took several calls and a trip halfway up the stairs before a muffled answer came from the room at the left of the stairway.

"Who is it?" Anitra asked as she came to the banister.

"I didn't ask. It's a girl and she's *waiting.*"

Dalice thought her mother had left the kitchen until

she heard a clatter from the broom closet. She looked around in time to see a dustpan skid across the floor and then a broom handle clacked and bounced on the floor.

"Having trouble?"

"Oh, you know me!" her mother said. She was holding a bottle of furniture polish, a wall brush, and a roll of paper towels. "Always trying to carry a lazy man's load because I don't want to make two trips."

"Mom! No one would ever accuse you of being lazy — not anyone who knows you."

Eileen Cornell smiled as she set the cleaning supplies on a chair. "Evidently you're saying I'm sort of on the brisk side?"

"I'd say so! You can tell it's Saturday by what you had in your arms."

"I'm not sure that's true. I sometimes clean during the week."

"Is this bacon for me?" Dalice asked.

"And your sister. Was that call for her?"

"Yes. She's down," Dalice replied as she dropped a slice of Golden Wheat bread into a slot of the toaster. "It's someone new. She called me Alice."

Eileen Cornell filled a glass of orange juice from a tall pitcher and set it on the table. "I often smile when I remember how your father and I debated over what to call you. Oh, we knew we would give you your grandmothers' names. But the problem was, which should be first? Either way one of our mothers might be hurt."

"Were they?"

"No. Simply because your father's mother, Alice, is not as touchy as mine. But that's not why we put Enid first. We'd repeat the names over first one way, — Alice Enid, then the other, Enid Alice. To tell the truth, I never liked the combination too well whichever way it was arranged. Then when Anitra came along and put the names together — well Dalice seems right to me."

"And to me," Dalice said. She cut the toast into triangles after spreading the slice with strawberry jam. She looked up at the window as she munched. "Isn't the world beautiful this morning?"

"Well, I suppose it is. But mainly I thought about the shoveling and sweeping that needs to be done when snow falls. And of how slippery the walks might be. I need to go to market. And as your Granddad Cranor always said to me, I'm as awkward on ice as a cow with a crutch."

Anitra came into the kitchen and thudded down on a chair. "I'm furious. The whole day's ruined for me."

"Who's responsible for that?" her mother asked.

"This weather. This lousy snow. Such klunky luck. Janie's mother was going to take us shopping — to Ravenwood. Now she's afraid to drive."

"Where's Ravenwood and who's Janie?" Mrs. Cornell asked.

"Janie's the new girl. I told you about her, about her father being the new superintendent of schools."

"You said this Dr. Spencer had a daughter your age. But you didn't even know her name night before last. And now you've made plans to go to — to some place. Shouldn't you have asked permission?"

"I was going to. Naturally. But now the whole thing's off. And everyone says Ravenwood's fabulous. Scads of stores."

"Then Ravenwood's a shopping center?"

"Yes. Over by Fort Wayne."

"How'd you make friends with this new girl in such a short time?" Mrs. Cornell asked.

"I offered to show her around. *After* Dana said she meant to be the one. But even if the trip's off I'm still *in* with Janie. She wants me to come over."

"Over where?"

"Not too far. To Brewington Woods."

"Well, I guess it's all right. After you do your work chart."

"Oh, Mother, that same old drag. Doing the slavery bit."

"Anitra Jo Cornell! You are not a slave. And don't start that worn argument about being the only girl who's expected to help out at home. I've talked to other mothers. And besides, what goes on in this house is not dependent on what other people think or do." She turned to Dalice. "What do you have planned for today?"

"I'm not exactly sure. For one thing I'm going to take a walk in this winter wonderland. Maybe I'll go to the library on the way to the mall. Daddy might be able to use some help at the store."

"Good idea," her mother said. "Especially about the store. The book business is picking up now that Thanksgiving's over."

Dalice felt that her sister was looking at her. She looked up to see the glare in Anitra's brown eyes. *What is she angry about? What have I done?* Then she realized. *Mama approved of my plans and questioned hers. Things like that seem to make her edgy — like Mom described Grandma Enid.*

"It's time for me to get busy," Dalice said. Her sister's attitude made her uneasy.

"Good old Dalice," Anitra said, "all noble and dutiful."

"Anitra!" Eileen scolded. "Sometimes your teasing is a little too sharp — even mean. You sounded as if you were making fun of Dalice. And I *won't* allow *that*, not from anyone!"

"Oh, Mother!" Anitra said. "You never could tell the difference between for fun and for serious. Can't a person even joke around here once in awhile?"

She wasn't teasing, Dalice thought. *She was glaring at me, almost like she hated me. But I don't want to think that's how she really feels.* She went to the closet and pulled the vacuum cleaner to the living room. For the first time she allowed her mind to dwell on something she'd not wanted to believe. *Is Anitra jealous of me? That's hard to believe. She's prettier than I'll ever be. I can see that and know other people do. Her grades were as high as mine until last year when she quit working hard. But why else is she irritated when anyone says nice things to me? It's like she feels put down when I'm approved of by anyone. Is this my fault?*

Dalice shook her head as if to clear it of puzzling thoughts. *I'll have to think about this later.* Sometimes she put problems on shelves, leaving them to be solved at some other time. *"That's the way Grandma Cornell does her jigsaws*, she remembered. *Says pieces fit together in her mind before she can put them in place on the card table.*

Dalice thought about her sister's actions. As she worked she couldn't keep the problem out of her mind. She thought back over the past few months. *Anitra's been a lot more hateful lately. She pouts a lot now. She never used to stay in her room as much as she does now. Usually she was on the phone.* Then Dalice realized how much things had changed. *This call this morning from the new girl was the first for a long time. Why?*

Dalice thought of asking her mother if she'd noticed that almost no one called her sister. *But it seems a little disloyal. It might look like I was meddling. And if Mom said anything to Anitra — and let on that I'm wondering — she would really be furious.*

2

DALICE checked off each of the chores on her list before eleven o'clock. She'd have finished sooner if she hadn't stopped to sort through the records to find all the Christmas albums. She dusted to the rhythm of "Jingle Bells," lined shelves while humming the melody of "Silent Night," and it seemed a lovely coincidence that she was buffing the knives and forks when the automatic changer dropped "Silver Bells" to the turntable.

Sometimes Dalice caught glimpses of what her Grandma Cornell meant when she said, "We exist in the world of our thoughts. So I try to shut the door on the unpleasant mental intruders." *Maybe I'm like her in some ways. Like when I watch summer rain make silver windows on the screen wire and wink out in the breeze. Or when maple leaves fall from the trees and look like autumn kites.*

Her mother was kneading egg-yellow dough with the heel of her hand when Dalice took the cleaning supplies to the kitchen. "We having noodles today?"

"No. I'm freezing these. The price of eggs is going up every week. No telling what it'll be by Christmas."

Dalice was trying to decide whether to postpone her walk until after lunch when her mother said, "You were rushing things a little, weren't you — playing Christmas records?"

"It seemed right," Dalice said. "With the snow. Besides, I like to have the feeling as long as I can." She almost added, "Don't you?" But she knew how her mother felt — or how she talked. She complained about the time it took to send cards, and worried if they got one from someone she'd dropped from her list. And she debated for days about what gifts to buy.

Sometimes Dalice wondered if her mother was — and she didn't like even the thought that she might be — selfish, or a little stingy. *Yet she gives lovely gifts, and keeps running out to buy extras. I'm wrong,* concluded Dalice. *I shouldn't even think ideas like that. Dad often says that if Christmas were postponed a week he'd have to put another mortgage on the house.*

Probably Mom does her thinking aloud. Like Anitra. Whatever comes to their mind they say. I keep most of my feelings to myself — unless I'm with certain people — like Daddy and Grandma Cornell or my close friend, Nancy Morrison.

14

Dalice looked at the yellow-faced clock above the sink. "Is it all right if I go now?"

"Before you eat?"

"Well, it hasn't been long since breakfast. I'll stop for a malt and a cheeseburger. Or maybe Daddy will treat me to a Coney Island."

"Has your sister gone?"

"I don't think so. I haven't heard any sounds since she went back upstairs."

"That child! Do you suppose she's gone back to bed? She surely realizes that she has to do her work before she goes to visit that new friend of hers."

Dalice didn't answer. Anitra often promised to do her share of the work later, but that time didn't come until there were other things to do.

I don't think I'll go upstairs. This skirt and turtleneck are clean and dressy enough for where I'm going. She pulled her high boots from the hall closet and brushed the dust from the brown leather. She checked her purse and found a dollar and seventeen cents left from her allowance. *That'll be enough. Especially if Daddy buys my lunch.*

The front walk hadn't been shoveled and Dalice had to take giant steps to match her footprints with her father's. Some sections of the sidewalk, which ran from the Cornells' end of Locust Avenue to the bus stop, were clear.

Dalice stopped to help Susie and Bruce Hinckley roll a snowball to a spot in front of the bay window of their home. "We want it there so we can sit and watch people stare when they see how big *our* Frosty is," Susie said.

"But it's not big *yet*," said Bruce. "Will you help us

15

lift the middle on the bottom, Dalice?"

"I'll help. But how about the head? You can't reach that high."

"Yes I can," the little boy said. "With the step stool. Mom let us borrow it. Come on, Susie. Push! Quit goofing off."

Dalice looked first at one child, then the other. They were so different. Susie was laughing as she pushed on the ball of snow. "See, Dalice! My feet slide back while I push frontwards. I'm all stretched out."

Bruce was more serious. *It's like making this snowman is his lifework*, thought Dalice. *They're so different — maybe as much as Anitra and I. Is it always that way in families? If so, it's a wonder there's not more fighting than there is.*

By the time Dalice reached the bus stop she'd decided to go straight to the mall and not stop at the library until she was on her way home. Being out in the crisp, frosty air and rolling snowballs had made her hungry.

Most of the streets were cleared either by snow sweepers or by the friction of moving traffic. But the bus driver had trouble pulling away from curbs after stopping for passengers. Dalice could feel the vibrations of spinning wheels and hear the snorting of the motor.

The parking lot of the shopping center was nearly full. *Daddy always says bad weather means more business for the mall. People like going from store to store without getting wet or cold, whether they buy much or not.*

Dalice loved the way she felt when she walked into Stuarts. It was one of a chain of bookstores and her

Susie and Bruce are so different, Dalice thought. *Maybe as much as Anitra and I. Is it always that way in families?*

father was the manager of this one. Since there hadn't been a bookstore in town for a few years, except by the university on the west side, people seemed to be ready for one. Sales had grown from a trickle to a stream, and Christmas buying made it into a torrent.

"Hello, there," the lady at the cash register said. "I thought we might see your smiling face today."

"Busy, Mrs. Norman?"

"Rushed is a better word. And I'm — or whoever's at the register — is the bottleneck. We need two today."

"Can I help?"

"Well, you'd better ask your father. He's unpacking in the storeroom. Jennie's out to lunch and Wayne's hunting a book on candlemaking."

Dalice edged past customers and around racks and shelves. She heard her father whistling his off-key version of "Star Dust." She knew he felt hurried or he would not have been out of tune. "Read any good books lately?" she asked him.

David Cornell looked up from the box of books after he'd slit the brown tape which joined the top flaps. "Who has time to read?"

"You do — but not today. Right?" Dalice said. "Can I help?"

"You can. By putting books in bags, to give Mrs. Norman more time to ring up sales. But — have you eaten?"

"No. Not since breakfast."

"Here — take this dollar and get a sandwich. I'd give you more, but I don't want you to stay long."

Dalice worked until three-thirty when Steve, a college student, came in. He and Jennie would take turns at the check-out counter until closing time.

Dalice barely had time to look at customers and did not get to flip the pages of a single book. "Don't figures swim before your eyes at night?" she asked Mrs. Norman.

"No. Not now. Not like they did at first. But I'll tell you what I do now and then. When the phone rings at home I answer by saying, 'Is this all for you?' That question's sort of tape-recorded in my mind."

Dalice stopped at the glassed-in cubicle that was her father's office. "You coming home for dinner?"

"I doubt it. Mrs. Norman's leaving at four and there doesn't seem to be much of a break. Maybe at five I'll let the others eat. Would you have your mother call me? Maybe all of you can come here to eat."

"I'll tell her. But I'll probably stay at home. I think Nancy's going to spend the night — *if* her parents go to Chicago."

"Well. It's been a big boost to have you here. You're not old enough to be on Stuarts' payroll. But you're on mine. Here's a small thank you," he said handing her three dollar bills.

"I'd work for you without pay."

"I know. I know," her father said as he rubbed one knuckle up and down on her cheek.

Dalice felt a rush of tenderness. Her father looked unusually weary. *But even now he's the handsomest man I've ever met. And the kindest.*

David Cornell's gray-green eyes searched her face. "Something on your mind?"

Dalice hadn't thought of the possibility that Anitra was jealous for several hours. Her father's question brought it to the surface of her mind. She wanted to say what she was thinking. *But there's not time and perhaps I shouldn't. It'd be disloyal and Daddy might worry and be cross with Anitra. Then she would lash out at me.*

"No. Nothing serious. If there is, you'll hear."

"Well, I hope so. Otherwise I'd wonder if you'd re-signed from the privileged and top-notch position of being my older daughter."

Dalice stopped at Tiffany's and bought four cream puffs for two reasons. *If Nancy comes and Mom eats out I'll have dessert. That's one reason for such a splurge. The other is that I love these sugar-dusted pastries.*

It was nearly dark when she got off the bus and hurried down Locust Avenue. She hadn't taken time to browse in the library, but she checked out two refer-ence books to use for her history report.

The walk was clear of snow and the porch lantern was glowing. *I wonder if Nancy called. She wasn't sup-posed to until five-thirty.* Lights were on in her par-ents' bedroom. *Mother must be going to meet Daddy. Will Anitra go along?* She couldn't help thinking that the evening would be more fun if her sister weren't around. But she shook her head as if to clear it of the selfish suggestion. *I'm making my plans and Anitra has a right to make hers — if Mom says yes.*

She glanced up and down the street as she slipped her feet from her boots. Lights were on in almost every house, making windows into gold rectangles and squares. The light from the lampposts along the street made the snow sparkle like glittering silver in the night. *The world looks beautiful — the part that I see now anyway.*

3

"WHERE IS EVERYONE?" Dalice called as she took her boots to the closet under the stairs. Two voices answered.

"Up here," her mother said.

"In here," Anitra responded from the room the Cornells called the Bee-Hive because it was the busiest room in the house. Eileen Cornell ironed and sewed and typed in it. Her husband had a roll-top desk in one corner and sat under the gooseneck lamp many nights, going over invoices, writing checks, and making up regular and special orders. Sometimes Anitra set up a card table and worked on her charcoal drawings. Dalice studied in the Bee-Hive only when the other

21

Cornells were not buzzing around.

"What are you drawing now?" Dalice asked as she stopped in the doorway. Anitra didn't like people peeking over her shoulder, and Dalice understood the feeling.

"Oh, something I saw as I came in the back gate. Little birds huddled on the branches of the redbud tree. Their feathers were all fluffed out."

"They're probably cold and maybe hungry," Dalice said.

"Not now. I put out some bread crumbs."

"May I see your drawing?"

"Sure. But I don't like it. The sparrows don't look cold, just mussed up and straggly. Besides, I have to run and change."

"You going with Mother?"

"Naturally. I'm too young to have special privileges like you."

"Now, Anitra. I'm sure Mother would let you stay at home."

"Well, I guess. But I'm going to get some new boots. High ones. White, I hope!"

Dalice picked up the linen-like paper on which her sister had sketched the birds on the bare branch. *She's really good. I wish she'd work harder at it. I've never understood why she decided not to take art in school this year.*

She took the cream puffs to the kitchen and looked around to see if her mother had cooked anything for her meal. She took a quilted pot holder from a brass hook and lifted the lid of a red enamel pan. *Yummy. Vegetable soup. A real cold-night treat.*

She heard her mother coming downstairs, calling

back, "Now hurry, Anitra. We're already late. Or will be by the time we get to the mall."

"You going to drive?" Dalice asked.

"Yes. The streets are clear. I called several people who live at various points across town."

"Did Nancy call?"

"No. She didn't. Do you want to change your mind and go with us?"

"No. I've been gone all day. And even if Nancy does not come I have some books, some to read for fun and others to study. *And* I wouldn't exchange your soup for anything I can think of right now."

"Well, thank you for the compliment. We won't be gone long. Not much over an hour and a half, or maybe two."

Dalice was dipping soup into a peach-colored bowl when the doorbell rang. She turned on the porch light and pulled the curtain back a few inches, following instructions not to unlock the door until she knew who was outside. She saw Nancy's bright red coat and long knitted scarf.

"Come in. I've been waiting to hear from you."

"Well, I tried — and I tried — and I tried! But your line was always busy. I began to wonder if the receiver had been knocked from its cradle."

Dalice turned to look as she reached out for Nancy's coat. "No. It's in place. Mom made several calls. But she has a thing about staying on the line. Usually doesn't talk more than five minutes. She says it's a holdover from the days when she was on an eight-party line. Come to the kitchen. You haven't eaten, have you?"

"No. We never do until seven. And my family left

at four. They'll eat at the airport, I guess."

The girls decided to put soup and dessert on trays and eat in front of the television. They wanted to watch the ice-skating competition. Dalice made hot tea during one station break and refilled the soup bowls during another.

After the evening news came on, Dalice flicked the switch and the girls talked for nearly an hour. They'd been friends since the Cornells moved to the city from Oakville, a small town fifteen miles away. Nancy was the first person in the class to ask Dalice her name. And that was the first time Dalice went on record with the contraction of her name. In the small town where almost everyone knew both her grandmothers and remembered when she was born she was usually called "Alice," but sometimes "Enid Alice."

"Where did your brothers stay?" Dalice asked as they carried dishes to the kitchen.

"Oh, they went along. And I could have. But for some reason these trips don't seem as exciting anymore. Not even as much as last year. I don't know why I've changed."

"Your folks do go real often," Dalice said. "Maybe you're bored with bowling tournaments."

"I don't think it's that. I mean sometimes it's fun. But I keep edging away from so much family togetherness."

"My mother would say it's our age showing."

"She would? Mine doesn't understand. I had to coax for a day and a half to get to stay here," Nancy said.

"That probably doesn't seem very exciting to her. Say! We haven't talked about tomorrow. About what we'll do. Anything in mind?"

"Why worry? It's fun not to know sometimes. We Morrisons have every weekend planned all year. It's like our family life is a bus schedule."

"Well, I know what I have to do right now. My bus hasn't been regular today. I don't have our bed made. In the carpenter shop."

"In the — Oh, you mean the room at the back."

The Cornell family had bought their story-and-a-half house from the original owner who'd made half the back porch, the northwest corner, into a workshop. The walls were of old wood, weathered gray by winds and rain. A heavy plank bench ran along the back wall under two one-sash windows. Eileen Cornell often talked about making it over either into a spare bedroom or a family room. But she usually added, "Our budget hasn't stretched to that corner of the house."

Dalice had turned the valve of the steam radiator that morning in case Nancy came. Before doing so she'd asked Anitra if *she'd* sleep on the couch.

"Why should I?" Anitra had said. "You get to have company a lot more than I do."

"I doubt that," Dalice replied. "But forget it. I don't want Nancy in here if you're going to be snippy. I'll clean up the carpenter shop."

"I didn't know you had a bed back there," Nancy said as she took the two pillows Dalice handed her from the hall closet.

"We didn't until my Grandmother Cranor was going to junk her old brass bed. I love it. So Mother said we'd store it out here until I was ready to use it. And this is the time — for one night, anyway."

The other three members of the Cornell family came home before eight o'clock. Anitra bubbled with excitement. "See, Dalice, I did get white ones. Aren't they absolutely delish?"

"How could boots be delicious?" Eileen Cornell said. "That's an adjective that is used in connection with eating."

"Once an English teacher, always an English teacher," David Cornell said. "You've taken on an impossible task, Eileen. Trying to correct the way kids use the language today."

"I'm not trying with all of them, just this one."

"How about Dalice? I suppose you think she's a grammar book walking around on two legs?" Anitra asked.

Dalice looked at her father. He frowned. *I hope he doesn't scold Anitra. Not in front of Nancy.*

"I think I'll pop some corn, whether anyone eats any or not," Eileen Cornell said. "It goes with a snowy evening."

"Next thing we know you'll have us stringing it for Christmas tree decorations," Dalice's father said. "That and cranberries."

"Not tonight. Not the berries, for one basic reason. We don't have any. But I would like to have an old-fashioned tree sometime. Get away from so much glitter."

"Oh Mother!" Anitra exclaimed. "Such an ancient idea."

A good idea's always good," her mother said.

One and one half television programs later Dalice asked Nancy if she was ready to go to bed. "I'm having trouble keeping my eyes open. Need props."

"All who believe that stand on their heads," David Cornell said with a twinkle in his eyes. "You girls will be talking until midnight."

"Not unless I wake myself up getting ready for bed."

The two girls did talk for nearly an hour. The light from the backyard lamppost cast a wide beam slantwise over the room. Dalice tipped her head so she could see the scrolls on the head of the brass bed and even some snail-curled knotholes in one wall.

"I like this room," Nancy said. "I wish it were in my house. I'd beg until I got it for my own."

"You mean like it is?"

"Sure! The bench would be a dressing table and these walls could be rubbed with something to make the grain stand out. My mother uses such stuff when she antiques furniture."

Dalice sat up in bed and hugged her knees. "That's a super idea! Why didn't I ever think of it?"

"Well, I guess you needed the benefit of my inspiring presence."

Dalice reached back and grabbed her pillow. "This will keep you from being too puffed up," she said as she threw it at Nancy. "But seriously, I'm going to ask if I can move in here."

"Do you really want a room of your own? I mean, sometimes I wish I had a sister, someone to share things with."

"Well, Anitra and I aren't that close. Not now anyway. We used to be. I'm not sure when things began to change. Or why."

"Do you fight?"

Dalice thought of the twins who'd been in the Sunday school class she taught until they graduated into the intermediate group. "Do you fight?" she had asked one morning. "Do twins ever get cross with each other?"

27

"I don't," Rhonda had answered. "Robin just fights with me."

That's how I feel about Anitra now, Dalice thought.

"Not really," she answered Nancy. "Mainly because I don't like fights or arguments. I'm a real pacifist, I guess, inwardly as well as on the outside. But I suppose even if you got along great with someone there'd be advantages to having a room of your own."

"There are," Nancy said.

"I can think of at least ten without straining my brain. And anyway, one problem's solved. I haven't known what I wanted for Christmas. Now I do. Whether I get it or not, I know."

4

DALICE wanted to bring up the subject of making the carpenter shop her room the first thing the next morning. But she knew there'd be a lot of discussion and it wouldn't be polite to involve Nancy in a family conference. *Besides, it'd be better if I got all of my in-favor arguments in order first.*

The Cornells and Nancy went to church, stopping at the Morrisons' house long enough to feed Scamp, their black and brown terrier. After services were over David Cornell offered to take everyone out to eat. "No," Eileen said. "You eat out everyday. And I have minute steaks ready to broil, potatoes baking in foil — thanks to the timer — and pie for dessert."

"Say no more," David said. "I've yielded to temptation. And I'd much rather be at home."

"Aren't we going anyplace today?" Anitra asked. "Is this going to be just another dull Sunday?"

"I'm sure you can find something to do," Eileen said. "We're not exactly isolated."

The red circle of the stoplight was bright when they came to the intersection of Jackson Street and Locust Avenue. Two girls stepped from the curb and crossed in front of the car.

"That's Dana," Dalice said. "She's waving, Anitra."

"I saw her — them," Anitra said. "I *waved*."

"Who is the girl with her?" Eileen Cornell asked. "Should I recognize her?"

"It's Jane Spencer."

"Oh. The one you visited yesterday. Such beautiful red-gold hair."

Dalice looked across Nancy at her sister. Anitra was biting one corner of her lower lip. *She's upset. Why? Because Dana's with the new girl?*

After lunch the three girls washed and put away the dishes. Dalice volunteered, Nancy insisted, and Anitra said she'd help. "Well," Eileen said, "I'm not the kind to turn down an offer like that. I think I'll run across the alley and see Miss Kathleen. I've neglected her lately."

"Do you mean Miss Manor?" Nancy asked as she watched the stream of water turn the detergent into a mountain of bubbles. "The one who taught?"

"Yes," Eileen said. "She came from my hometown. I was one of her students. We all called her Miss Kathleen because everyone knew her."

"I had her too," Nancy said. "Doesn't she go out?"

"Oh yes," Eileen answered. "In fact, I may not find her at home. She doesn't drive but goes whenever she's invited, which is often. Says she's not always in the mood to go but that maybe no one would ask her when she was."

Anitra had little to say as she put the good china in the closet and stored the silver in its walnut chest. She wasn't sharp or even sulky — just quiet. When Dalice suggested a walk, she agreed to go along. "Walking's not my favorite thing, and I don't want to go far, but there's not much else going on around here."

The girls crossed Jackson and kept going until they came to Christy Woods. "We could go in," Dalice said. "The university opens the greenhouse to visitors on Sunday afternoons. I'd love to see the orchid collection again."

"I think I'll go back," Anitra said.

"Why?" Nancy cheerfully asked. "Aren't we good company?"

"It's not that. I saw some birds through the fence and they made me think of something I have to do at home."

"Okay, but you'd better not go someplace else," Dalice reminded her, "without telling Mom first."

"Don't worry, Big Sister."

"What did she mean?" Nancy asked. "What was that about birds?"

"A drawing," Dalice said. "I saw it. She's really good. But she didn't take art this year. I don't know why."

It was four o'clock before the girls returned to the Cornells' house. Eileen relayed the message that the

Morrisons were back in town and Nancy got ready to leave. "I've had a terrific time, Mrs. Cornell. Thanks for girl-sitting me."

"It's been good to have you with us," Eileen said. "I hope you didn't feel unwelcome because you had to sleep in our storeroom."

"Oh, no. I loved it back there." Nancy glanced at Dalice and winked. "Dalice knows I do."

After Nancy left, Dalice said, "I'd better do my homework. This weekend has seemed so *short*. Are we doing anything tonight?"

"Not much," her mother said. "Except that I invited Miss K to come over and eat with us. At six-thirty."

"Then I'll have time to finish my assignments. Where did Anitra go?"

"She's in the Bee-Hive, I think."

Darkness came and her desk lamp had been on for over thirty-five minutes when Dalice heard three raps on the door. She didn't need to look to know who was there. "Come in, Mom."

"Finished?"

"Almost. What's on your mind?"

"Curiosity. I caught a signal when we were talking about the carpenter shop — before Nancy left. What were you two *not* saying?"

Dalice put the cap on her felt-tip pen and pushed her notebook back on the desk. "You know what Daddy would say, don't you? That your antenna was pointing in the right direction."

But I don't know the code. What *was* the message?"

"I don't know how you'll feel. And maybe you'll

say no. It could be that — "

"Dalice! What are you trying to say?"

"That what I want for Christmas is to have the carpenter shop for my room."

"You're *serious*?"

Dalice nodded. "The idea came from Nancy. But I liked it then, and the more I think about it the better it seems."

"Well, I don't know what to say," Eileen said. "At least not until I talk to your father. Mainly because of the expense for paneling and things."

"That's what you may not understand." Dalice explained that she liked the look of the weather gray walls and that the work bench could be both a bookshelf and a dressing table. "I know the heating would take more money. And the floor would need something. But Mom, I have the brass bed. And I'm sure we could use that storage cupboard for my clothes."

Eileen promised that they'd discuss the matter. "But not tonight. Miss Kathleen is due any minute."

Now that she'd spoken of the idea of having her own room, Dalice's mind whizzed with plans and possibilities. *What color would go with gray?* Pink seemed natural, and not only because it was her favorite color. The words gray, pink, and gold made a picture. *I could make pillows, patchwork maybe, and dye something like old sheets for draperies. Surely Mom will say I can bring my desk down if I need it. Anitra wouldn't want two.*

The thought of her sister squelched some of Dalice's enthusiasm. *What will she say? Maybe nothing. She could be glad to have our room to herself. But ac-*

tually she's never complained much about what I do, not when we're alone. It's only around others that she gets more spiteful. I wonder why?

The Cornells and their guest were eating toasted cheese sandwiches when the telephone rang. No one moved until the third ring, then they glanced toward Anitra. "What's wrong, Anitra Jo?" Mrs. Cornell asked. "You aren't jumping and running."

Dalice volunteered to answer but she had time to hear Anitra say, "It's not anyone for me."

How can she know that? Has something happened? Dalice thought as she crossed the hall. The call was for her father. "Daddy," she said, "Wayne wants to know if you could use him early at the store tomorrow."

"I'll talk to him," David Cornell said.

"My goodness," Miss Kathleen said as Dalice went back to the table. "I almost envy you people even if envy *is* a sin. Having access to all those books. Not that I don't think the whole town's fortunate — having a store again. I get impatient with myself for not making the effort to get out there."

"You mean you've not been to the mall?"

"No. Isn't that backward of me? But changing buses seems like a lot of trouble and taxis are so expensive."

"David," Eileen said as her husband came back to the table, "Miss K's never been out to the mall."

"We'll take care of that. You bring her down one day this week. Before I go home from work, I'll show her around."

"Well, I wouldn't want to impose," Miss Manor said. "Didn't mean to hint."

"You *wouldn't*," Eileen answered.

Dalice had trouble keeping her mind on cheese sandwiches. Her eyes saw the plate but her thoughts were back in the carpenter shop. She wondered when her mother would discuss the idea with her father. *Even if she brings it up tonight, I won't hear what he thinks until later. Will I get a chance to say how I feel before they say no?*

Anitra went to their room first and was on her bed reading when Dalice went upstairs. "New books?"

"No. One of my favorites."

"I see now. Mom's Cherry Ames books. I read them over too. Maybe I shouldn't ask, Anitra, but is something bothering you?"

"What makes you think *that*?"

"Oh, I don't know. Just a feeling. Mainly because of what you said when the telephone rang. Since when won't anyone call you? You get more than anyone, unless it's Daddy — when he's home."

Anitra turned over with her face to the wall. "I don't want to talk about it."

Talk about what? Is she about to cry? What has happened? Dalice wanted to go over and touch her sister as she would have when they were younger and she didn't understand what kept her from following that impulse. *What happens to people? Even those in the same family? Two or maybe three years ago I'd have known why Anitra was upset without asking. Who's changed? Or what?*

She read a chapter in her American history textbook before getting ready for bed. Her mother came to the door to say good-night. Anitra answered her but didn't reply when Dalice said, "Happy dreams."

Is she asleep, or only pretending?

The steam radiator hissed now and then and the pipes clanked when the thermostat turned on the heat. Otherwise the house was still until Dalice heard what had to be a muffled sob. She raised up on one elbow and tried again, "Happy dreams, Anitra."

Her sister didn't answer.

5

THE WIND woke Dalice the next morning. It shook the windowpanes and whistled around the corner of the house. *It sounds fierce*, Dalice thought. *Are we going to have a blizzard?* She sat up in bed and looked out the window. Not a snowflake in sight.

She glanced at her watch. *Seven-fifteen. Did Mother call me?* She hurried to the closet and took out her gray and red plaid skirt and the turtleneck sweater that matched the crimson. "Time to get up, Anitra," she said as she started toward the bathroom.

"I'm not going to school," Anitra replied.

"What's the matter? Did Mom say you could stay home?"

"I feel terrible, like I'm getting something. Mom doesn't know yet. Tell her, will you?"

"Well I'll *tell* her. But she'll come up and check. You know that."

"Just *tell* her," Anitra said as she pulled the blue and white quilt over her head.

Is she playing sick? Does this wanting to stay at home have something to do with her crying last night? If she was.

Eileen Cornell was in the living room reading the morning newspaper. "No breakfast this morning? Is our cook on strike, maybe" Dalice asked. She'd stopped in front of the hall mirror to put the tortoise shell clasp around the section of hair which fluffed out into a ponytail.

"The first shift has already eaten. Your father expects an early delivery at the store. Is Anitra about ready to come down?"

"She's not even up. Says she doesn't feel like going to school."

"She doesn't? I'd better take her temperature. The oatmeal's simmering in the double boiler."

Dalice had finished eating before her mother came downstairs. "She doesn't have a fever. But she insists she isn't well enough to go. So! I guess I'll let her stay at home. *But* if she slips down to watch TV or use the phone, off to school she'll go."

"Who would she call, Mom?" Dalice asked. "Everyone's at school."

"Unless *they* are pulling the wool over *their* mothers' eyes."

Dalice didn't think of asking if her parents had talked about her idea of having a room of her own

Is Anitra playing sick? Dalice wondered. *Does it have some-thing to do with her crying last night?*

until she was half a block from home. Her mind was on Anitra *I don't think she's really sick. But there has to be something wrong. She pouts a lot these days and tries to get her own way.*

Dalice was scared. She didn't want anything to happen to anyone, especially to Anitra. She'd always wanted to protect her curly-haired sister even when she was willful and thoughtless. Like the time at church when she'd seen Anitra break the strap on another girl's purse. The girl had cried and Anitra kept saying, "If *she* hadn't leaned back when I pulled, it wouldn't have come apart."

The girl's mother had called the Cornell home to protest. But Anitra said over and over, "It wasn't my fault."

Dalice had kept silent, but often wondered if she should have. When she heard her sister tell little lies to keep herself out of trouble, Dalice always thought, *A lot of kids do that. Sometimes I do too. And grownups aren't always truthful. But it's never right.*

Occasionally Dalice met Nancy Morrison at the corner of Jackson and Locust but neither waited if there was a reason why they had to be at school early or if the weather was bad. They didn't have to do everything together. Dalice had been half of such a friendship for the past year and a half before they moved from Oakville. Corinne Painter had wanted only one best friend at a time. At first Dalice had been comfortable with Corinne who was blond and blue-eyed, the prettiest girl in school. But after a while the friendship became an entangling web. It wasn't fun having a friend who was hurt if you walked to class with someone else or who asked whom you were talking to if she called and the line was busy. Dalice was not free of that web until the Cornells moved to the city. She'd been hurt and disappointed, but hadn't let Corinne's feelings influence her life in all areas.

Feelings of gratitude and appreciation filled Dalice's mind when she saw Nancy waiting at the corner. "It's too cold to stand out in this wind," she said.

"I just got here. Mother let me out when I saw your red coat. She's taking the boys to elementary."

"I was thinking about a girl I used to run around with. Remembering made me appreciate you."

"How so"

"Well, Corinne — she sort of possesses people. Does not like anyone she can't."

"I know. A lot of girls are like that. Inseparable for a while, then not speaking."

"I wonder why *we're* not?"

"I don't know why you're not," Nancy said, "but my own reason I know. I got dropped — way down — by someone whose loyalty I *never* doubted. That hurt. I cried and crawled into a shell. Miss Manor helped me out — out to the light."

"How? What did she say?"

"Well, you know she taught in our school. But you didn't go here then, did you? Anyway, I stayed in her room after class to study. I felt very lonely and sorry for myself. She came in and started talking. I can't remember all she said. But this one thing I'll never forget. She put her hand on my shoulder and said, 'Nancy, ask yourself, What am I supposed to learn from this? Trying to find that out eases the pain.' "

41

"I see," Dalice said. "And what you learned was not to get involved in possessive friendships. Right?"

"Right!"

Nancy went up one ramp and Dalice another when they reached the school building. They had only one class together and that was at the end of the day. But each often had to stay over for her own reasons and so rarely walked home together.

Dalice walked part way home with Scout Carson. She'd begun to have the feeling that he didn't leave the industrial arts wing until he saw her start home by way of the front door. If Nancy or any other girl was with her he either hurried ahead or lagged behind.

The Carsons had moved in from a small town in Randolph County about the same time the Cornells bought the house on Locust Avenue. The two families had met at a church reception for newcomers. For over a year all Dalice knew about the slender, dark-haired boy was that his nickname came from Kit Carson, the Indian scout, and that he was her age. He was shy, more so than most boys. She rarely saw him talking to girls in class.

"I haven't seen you for a while," Dalice said. "Been sick?"

"No. Busy. I'm a sack boy at the market over on White River Parkway."

"We go there sometimes. I didn't see you."

"Well, that's not surprising. I'm on the run a lot."

"Do you like it?"

"It's okay. But I wouldn't want to do this the rest of my life."

"What do you want to do?"

"I'm not sure. I keep changing my mind."

"So do I," Dalice said. "But what did you change from? And to?"

"For a long time I wanted to be a forest ranger. Now, with all this talk about ecology maybe I'll go into the soil conservation service or manage a state park."

"Would you have to go to college?"

"Sure. That's why I'm a sack boy now. And you?" They kept talking until they came to the intersection where Dalice had to turn onto Locust Avenue. *He's really ambitious*, she thought as she hurried along, ducking her head against the cold east wind. *I'm a little surprised. He looks so young compared to the guys with long sideburns and below-the-collar hairstyles.*

The aroma of cinnamon and baking yeast dough came to her as she opened the back door. "Yummy," she called. "Do I smell tea ring?"

"You do," her mother said as she pulled a long baking pan from the oven. "*And* I baked a sampler. It's there on that folded towel."

"Anitra downstairs?"

"No. She didn't come down."

"Is she really sick?"

"I'm still not sure. She ate well and has no fever. She'll either go to school tomorrow or to the doctor."

"She'll go to school — unless she really is getting something. She hates medicine, and shots petrify her. Me too — a little."

"When you go up — no, I've changed my mind. Do not ask her if she's coming down to eat. Tell her you will take up a tray. If she's pretending maybe she'll want to come down and watch TV."

"Mother, I can't help asking. Did you talk to Daddy about my room?"

"Yes, I did. He said he'd think about it and we'd discuss it tonight."

Anitra was awake and was sitting propped up on pillows. "You better?" Dalice asked.

"I guess. Did you see anyone in my class? Did they ask about me?"

"Where would I see anyone in your class?"

"Oh, at the Soda Shop or on the street."

"I didn't stop anyplace on the way home. And it's cold outside. No one's standing around anywhere. Why?"

"Oh, I just wondered."

"Want me to call Dana or someone? Ask for your assignments?"

"No. Don't call *her.* Besides, I'll probably have to go back tomorrow."

"What's wrong, Anitra? You've always liked school."

"That's what you think. Everyone's not a grind like you."

Dalice felt her ears getting warm. *Am I angry, or hurt or both?* "I was just asking. I want to help if I can."

She thought, *She's certainly getting snippy! Snaps at me even when we're alone. I don't know about me. Maybe I'm too meek. Too scared to get in a big old fight which she seems to want. Well! She'll have to wait. I have better things to do.*

6

ANITRA ate with the family and stayed downstairs to watch television. "I'll take your turn at doing dishes," Dalice said. She realized that she had her own reason for volunteering, and admitted that she was being a little selfish.

Her father lingered over the meal, saying he hadn't had time for lunch. "Wayne brought a sandwich to the back room and Mrs. Norman treated me to a pineapple crush sometime during the afternoon," he said.

"Were you that busy?" Eileen Cornell asked.

"Yes, both in front and back. The United Parcel truck came and left the storeroom stacked. There was barely room to walk between the cartons."

"Books you ordered?"

"Some we had, and others the home office want us to sell."

Dalice glanced first at her mother then her father as she polished a cut-glass dish. "You two ready to talk about my idea?" she asked.

.."I'm willing," her father said. "What's the problem?"

"Don't you think there are any?" Dalice asked. "I mean, I expected you to have six or seven reasons why the whole thing is out of the question."

"I can't think of one," David Cornell said. "Now if you'd taken a notion to have the room paneled, or if we didn't *have* extra space and you wanted a room built, then there'd be no use talking. Not this winter."

"I probably wouldn't have asked if that was what it took."

"Well, I hate to be the one to throw cold water on the plan," Eileen said. "But I see a problem."

"What's that?" Dalice asked.

"How — well, it seems to me it'll be unhandy to reach. At least chilly. You'll have to go through the back porch which isn't heated. And it doesn't seem safe — to have you set apart back there."

"We didn't even think of being afraid," Dalice said. "Nancy and I."

"But you weren't alone."

"Wait a minute," David said. "This part of the conversation is pointless. There *is* a door. From the Bee-Hive. You remember, Eileen, we boarded it up."

"That's right! I wanted you to make shelves in the space."

Dalice listened as her father talked. He said it'd be

a simple matter to rip out the boards. *But I would want a door for privacy,* she thought.

"I'd feel better about having her room open to the Bee-Hive," Eileen admitted. "I suppose I could hang a curtain.

"I'll do better than that. How would you like a louvered door? It'd look okay in both rooms. Or would it?"

"I'd like that," Dalice said. "And I'd want my side pink — very pale like the petals of wild roses. But, Daddy, you didn't say anything about the expense for extra heat."

"Well, there you're in luck. It's a good thing we still have a furnace that burns coal. That's one fuel that doesn't seem to be in short supply. It won't take many more chunks to heat the shop. Mr. Jackson told me he packed the walls tight with insulation."

By this time the dishes were put away and all three sat around the table. David Cornell listened as Dalice and her mother talked about furniture, curtains, and then rugs. When they came to the subject of floor covering he intervened. "How about that floor? What can we use on it?"

"I have the perfect solution," Eileen said. "Soap and water. I tried it on a spot today. With the dirt removed, the wide boards would look nice."

"I wish I could work out there right now," Dalice said. "I get so *impatient.* I wish I didn't sometimes."

"We'll get at the job this weekend," David Cornell said. "I'll do a little measuring tonight and go down to the department store tomorrow. They order things like the louvered door we need *and* you can get your pink paint there too, Dalice."

47

"I can't believe how this is working out. I was all prepared to do some arguing and tried to get ready to be disappointed," Dalice said.

"Parents aren't always unreasonable grouches," David Cornell said.

Dalice smiled and said, "I know. I *know*."

She thought of calling Nancy to tell her. Then she remembered. *Tonight's choir practice at their church. She'll be gone until six-thirty.* She went to the living room and sat down to watch the last part of the evening news.

Anitra was curled up on the end of the flowered couch. She was rolling her hair up on blue curlers. She rarely chose anything of another color.

"Why do you use those?" Dalice asked. "Your hair curls by itself."

"Not like I want," Anitra said. "Not tight and springy like Janie Spencer's. Say, I saw someone from your class on the local news. Linda West."

"What for? Oh, did she win the Citizenship Award?"

"Yes. For the whole state."

"That's great! I'm going to call her."

"Why are *you* so glad. Didn't you try for it?"

"Yes. Ten of us did the essay and filled out the questionnaire. But Nancy and I both thought Linda would get it."

"Why? You get good grades."

"I didn't expect to win," Dalice said. "Linda is involved in more activities. She's a candy striper. You know me! I'm more of a loner. Grandma Cornell told Mom once that it'd be a waste of time to enter me in a popularity race. That I wouldn't run."

"Don't you want to be popular?"

48

"Oh, I don't know. Not in the way people usually talk of being popular — like flitting from boy to boy and stuff."

"We *sure* are different," Anitra said. "I'd give anything to be in Linda's shoes. I mean anything."

Dalice looked at her sister and didn't like what she saw. *She looks hard — and all at once too grown up.* She went to the kitchen and asked, "Is it too late to go over to Nancy's after her choir practice?"

"You thinking of walking?"

"Yes. Why?"

"It's dangerous. A girl out by herself. I'll go along. Her mother and I are on the program committee for the *Book Club.* So you call and if they're free we'll go — but only for an hour."

It was nearly nine o'clock before Dalice and her mother started home. The wind had ebbed and the moon was a pale silver disk in the gray sky. The bushes and tree limbs were iced in night frost. "It's lovely outside, isn't it?" Dalice asked.

"And *cold.*"

"I know. But I like that too. The way the snow creaks under our feet and the sparkles of light on the whiteness."

"You are truly a winter girl, in more ways than one," her mother said.

"What do you mean? I like every season."

"I know. But it's easier to see the good about spring and summer and even fall. It is for me at least. But you find something warm and bright even in freezing and gloomy weather. I wish I were more like you."

"That's a switch," Dalice said. "I thought children were supposed to follow their parents' example."

49

"Not always. Not if it's not a good one," Eileen said.

Dalice put her arm around her mother's waist and said, "Don't put yourself down, Mother. You aren't one one hundredth as bad as you make yourself seem."

"Well, thank you. Sometimes I do redeem myself in my own eyes. By admitting that I'm wrong."

Anitra was still watching television. "You should be in bed, young lady," Eileen said. "I'm surprised that your father hasn't ordered you upstairs. Where is he?"

"Oh, out in the carpenter shop doing something. I heard pounding once or twice. Besides, I'm not sleepy. I slept hours today."

"Well you're going to sleep more hours tonight and go to school tomorrow."

Dalice went to the door of the Bee-Hive, wondering if her father had knocked the boards from the closed entrance to the carpenter shop. The wall was the same. So she hurried through the kitchen and back porch. A rush of warm air came out as she entered the rectangular room. "I thought you weren't going to do anything out here until the weekend."

"I'm not. Not much. Just ripping out shelves in one half of the storage closet to make room for your clothes which go on hangers. You know, Dalice, I see why you like the idea of having your room back here. I'm surprised we didn't think of it ourselves." He looked at his watch. "Well, I think I'll bring this day to an end. It'll soon be time to start another."

If Anitra wasn't asleep when Dalice went upstairs, she gave no sign that she was awake. Dalice didn't speak but she did a lot of thinking before the day ended for her. She thought of what her mother had said about some parents not being good examples to their children. She knew this was true and could see why there was a lot of rebellion against rules, because the people who made them broke them so often.

It gets a little scary, Dalice thought. *If kids do bad things because their parents do — and this keeps on and on, how can things ever get better?*

She tried to analyze her own thinking and actions. *I don't break rules very often. Not just because of who makes them. I feel safer, more protected, when I follow them. I'm lucky. Mom talks about her feelings, but she never sets a bad example. She never does anything that I'd get into trouble for doing.*

She raised herself up on her elbow and thumped at the pillow to make it fluffy before pulling the blanket and quilt up over her shoulders. She could see the bright full moon and the outline of the bare branches of the tall Lombardy poplar tree. *I'm truly lucky — and so is Anitra — if she only knew it.*

7

DALICE called her mother from school at noon the next day. "I meant to ask you this morning. Could you go to the mall after school? Either pick me up or meet me. To look at doors, I mean."

"Well, I *could*. But I'd really rather you and your father made that decision. I trust you. But the real reason is that your grandmother's coming to stay three days. Her church is having some kind of a convention. She'll be at the bus station at 3:20."

"Great! You go ahead and meet her. I may come home with Daddy. Depends on what time he's ready to leave."

"Please try to drag him away so we can eat by six.

There's a vesper session at 7:30 to open the convention."

Dalice had a bubbly feeling as she hurried to the cafeteria. So many good things were happening. It was exciting to plan for her own room and there were at least half a dozen things she wanted to do all at once. Knowing she could work in the bookstore when she had time was another plus. With Christmas coming the store would be unusually busy, and she would have a chance to earn money to buy gifts and things for her room. *And tonight Grandma will be there. That's always special. But we probably won't see much of her.*

Only five people were sliding dull orange trays along the steel poles in front of the cafeteria counter. *I must have talked longer than I realized,* Dalice thought. *I hope there's something left.* She turned down sauerkraut and wieners in favor of vegetable soup, carrot curls, and apple brown Betty. She'd tried to force herself to like kraut. *The eating I can manage. But liking — no way.*

She barely had time to finish her meal before the sound of the bell, warning that classes would begin in five minutes, jangled through the halls. *It's a good thing I don't know anyone in here. Talking would have kept me from having time for my dessert.*

She reached the locker at the end of school just as Nancy was closing hers. "Anything rushing on your schedule?"

"No," Nancy said. "I was going to wait and walk home with you if that's where you're going."

"It is. But not now. Say! Could you go with me to the mall? Call your mother?"

"I could call but no one would answer. The boys'
bowling league meets at Rose Lanes. Is there a special reason you're going?"

"There certainly is. I'll explain on the way. It's
about my room."

The girls had to wait twenty minutes until someone came to relieve Dalice's father at the check-out
counter. They went to the Ice Cream Corner for a
cone. "I don't want to get a sandwich," Dalice explained. "My grandmother's coming and I know Mother will have a big dinner."

"I don't know how it is to have a grandmother,"
Nancy said. "Not one that comes to see you or that
you visit."

"Aren't yours living?"

"One is. But she didn't want my father to get married — at least to Mom. So we're disowned, and she's
never met me or my brothers."

"Well," Dalice said, "if she isn't a loving person
you're probably better off."

"Are yours? Loving, I mean."

"Yes they are, I guess. But one shows it more than
the other — or maybe just in different ways."

"You sound as if you like one more than the other."

"I don't think so," Dalice said. "It's just that Grandma Cornell really seems to understand me. I guess
we're a lot alike. But with Anitra it's different. She
goes to see our other grandmother more often.
Grandma Cranor's her favorite."

"Are they alike?"

"Yes. Only I never thought about it much until
lately," Dalice answered. The idea that Anitra was

jealous kept coming to mind and she felt like she was biting her tongue to keep from putting it into words. For one reason — there wasn't time. Selecting the door and leafing through pages of paint chips took all the time they had.

Before Nancy got out of the car, Dalice said, "I want you to meet Grandma while she's here. I'll call you before she leaves town. She won't be around tonight."

As they drove the next three blocks Dalice told her father, "Nancy never knew either of her parents' mothers — not even the one who's alive. She asked me how it is to know them."

"How is it? To you?" David Cornell asked.

"Well, it's sort of hard to explain. But knowing my grandmothers helps me understand life — and even you and Mom. When I hear her tell about things you did when you were a little boy, I understand you better and feel closer."

"I know."

"You do?"

"Sure. I had grandmothers too."

A meal of chicken pot pie and buttered baby limas, with fresh fruit salad and chocolate chip cookies was waiting for them at home. Grandma Alice Cornell was wearing a crisp white apron over her rose dress. She managed to hug her son and granddaughter at the same time. "Let me feel your cold faces. I love that breath of outdoors."

Conversation was relished as much as food for nearly an hour. Alice Cornell told what was happening in Oakville. "They put shutters on the belfry of the church to keep the pigeons from nesting in the tower. In one way I was sad. I loved to see the birds soaring out from all sides when the custodian pulled the rope from below. But in another way it might be an improvement. Think how those birds must have felt when the clanging began."

"But they kept on going back," Dalice said.

"I know. They don't learn from experience like people do — or are *capable* of doing."

"How's the church doing?" Eileen Cornell asked.

"Sailing along rather smoothly, just a few ripples here and there. The storm over the last preacher — or the reactions of some folks to him — has died down. My goodness, Eileen, how do you get your crust so flaky?"

"Mother Cornell! It's your recipe."

The talk meandered from one subject to another. Dalice loved the word for wandering and winding movement. She'd followed the course of Stony Creek which ran along the bank of her Uncle Jim's farm and felt free and tranquil.

As Eileen served second helpings of the fruit salad Alice Cornell said, "We've covered the subject of Oakville. Now, what's going on here that I don't already know?"

At first no one spoke. *Maybe we're all trying to decide what she hasn't heard or are waiting for someone else to start*, Dalice thought.

"Well, business is good at the store," David Cornell said. "Even better than last year at this time."

For the first time during the mealtime Dalice looked directly at her sister. *She hasn't said a word. Just eats and hardly looks up — except when Grandma talked about the pigeons.*

Dalice's attention was brought back to the others when her father said, "You tell it, Dalice. The plans for your new room." For ten minutes the conversation stayed on one subject with Dalice doing most of the talking.

"I love even the thought of this room," Alice Cornell said. "*And* there may be some things in my attic you could use. The fan-backed wicker chair came to my mind."

"I remember it," Dalice said. "It was in the sunroom. I used to pretend it was a throne. It'd be perfect — only, would you want it painted pink?"

"I'd want it painted whatever color you choose. I'll have to see this room. Well, I guess I have — but not with you in mind."

"It still looks like a carpenter shop except in our imaginations," David Cornell said. "But we'd like to add your vision to ours."

"How about you, Anitra? Are you excited about having a room of your own?"

For a minute Dalice thought her sister was going to cry. She looked around the table and then tossed her head. "It's okay by me. At least Dalice's reading lamp won't be shining in my eyes all the time."

She's not saying how she really feels. She's upset, Dalice thought. *I can tell. I saw her chin quiver. Like it used to do when she was a little girl. Surely she doesn't feel bad because we won't be sharing a room. What is it then?*

After the girls' grandmother looked at the carpenter shop their father took her across town to the church. Anitra and her mother began to clear the table and wash the dishes. Dalice went upstairs for her pajamas and housecoat. She'd decided to sleep in the brass bed instead of on the living-room couch when she learned that her father had kept the heat on for the past two days. In a way she'd hoped to be in the room with her grandmother. They'd had many nighttime talks. *But perhaps it's better this way. Grandma has her meetings and will need to rest.*

As she went downstairs she heard her sister say in a choked voice, "I might as well not be in this family. For all any of you care."

"Anitra! You're overreacting," Eileen Cornell said. "I admit we should have been sure you knew about Dalice's room. I supposed you'd heard us talking. But I'm puzzled. Why *are* you so upset?"

Dalice sat down on the third from the bottom step. *My being in on this won't help.*

"Don't you want a room to yourself?" Eileen asked.

"Sure! What girl wouldn't? It's just that no one told me. Makes me feel like an outcast or something."

"But you were up in your room a lot. And watching television. After all, we haven't been talking about this for months or even weeks. Just two or three days. Do you think we should have asked you if you'd like the shop?"

"I wouldn't have it," Anitra said. "It's not my kind of thing."

"Then why. . .?"

Dalice waited for what seemed like five minutes before her sister answered. Several pieces of silverware clinked together before Anitra spoke. "Well, I guess I might as well come out and say it. I get tired of all the fuss being made over every little thing Dalice thinks and does."

58

I was right. She is jealous. Dalice folded her arms across her knees and rested her head on the crisscross. She felt sad. The girl she'd loved and wanted to protect was jealous of her. *Maybe I have been selfish part of the time,* Dalice thought. *What can I do to prove to Anitra that I really do care about her?*

She raised her head and listened as her mother said, "I think you're being unfair, Anitra. We love you equally and are just as proud of what you do as we are of Dalice's accomplishments."

"You're wrong there, Mom. As wrong as you can be. Do you want to know why? Well! I'll tell you. I don't do anything anyone can be proud of anymore."

Dalice was so startled that she didn't say a word when Anitra came running past her, on the way to her room. *I know something's wrong now. Someone should try to find out what it is. Anitra's miserable. Maybe because of her own jealousy, but still she's feeling terrible.*

8

WHEN DALICE went to the kitchen the next morning her grandmother was at the range and her mother was not in sight. "Did Mom oversleep?"

"Oh, no. She saw Miss Kathleen's light. And ran across the alley to ask her to eat pancakes and sausage with us. So she and I could have a little visit."

"Do you know her? Of course you do. Because she taught in Oakville."

"That's right. And I try to spend a little time with her when I come to Muncie. But she's not always at home and I usually have a full schedule. You're supposed to call your sister. I have six pancakes ahead — in the oven."

Anitra came to the head of the stairs at the first call. "Grandma has breakfast ready," Dalice said.

"I'm coming. Where's Mother? What's she doing?"

"She's at Miss K's. Why?"

"Oh, nothing. Well, actually I heard the phone ring and wondered who'd call so early."

"I don't know," Dalice said. "I can't hear it from the shop."

"It was for me!" David Cornell said as he came out of the bedroom. "From the home office. Mr. Miller wants me to go to Kokomo one day this week. See if I can figure out why that store's sales are down."

"Are you going?"

"I guess it's required. But I'm reluctant — sort of feel like a spy."

The grown-ups were still at the table when Dalice finished breakfast and headed for school. Anitra had left a few minutes earlier, saying she had to get a book from the library before she went to class.

Like almost every school day the hours seemed to race toward 3:15. For the most part, Dalice liked school. She knew there were problems, and that they were usually caused by people who had problems. She was aware that there were a few incidents caused by bad feelings between people of different races. She knew that there were times when snobbishness hurt some people and made them feel left out — mainly girls. She was even aware that some teachers were unfair, once in a while. But none of these wrongs kept school from being right for her.

A cold east rain stung her face as she left the building. Most of the snow was being washed away and the streets were covered with gray slush. It splattered out from the tires of passing cars. She walked so fast she was close to trotting. She looked for Anitra among the groups which came from the direction of the junior high school. None of the girls she saw wore long knit scarves of robin's-egg blue.

She went around the house to the back door. *No use to track up Mother's rug. I should've worn my boots.*

No one in sight. There were no dancing pans on the stove, no linen cloth nor any place mats on the round table. *That's strange,* she thought. *Unless Grandma's not coming back here to eat — or we're going out for some reason.*

"Dalice? I'm in the Bee-Hive," her mother called.

As Dalice walked in the door she saw her mother standing at the one long window. Rain streamed down the top pane in shimmering waves. "Why are you in here? Been working on something?"

"In my mind, yes," Eileen Cornell turned and swallowed hard. Her mother's eyes were red and her face puffy and splotchy from crying.

"What's wrong, Mom? Is someone hurt?"

"No. No. Nothing like that. Sit down here at the card table and I'll tell you as much as I can now. Anitra's upstairs and she'd be hurt if she thought I was discussing this with you. In fact, she said. 'Don't go blabbing this to Dalice.'"

Questions and guesses circled and bumped into one another in Dalice's mind, but she waited for her mother to go on. "I was called to school today for a conference with the counselor. Anitra — well, she has problems. And her grades are going down — way down. I don't see why I didn't notice. Why did I have to be told?"

Dalice saw her mother standing at the one long window. "What's wrong," Dalice asked, "is someone hurt?"

"Do they know why she's having trouble?"

Her mother nodded, and bit her lower lip before she spoke. "They think so and that's why I'm upset, worried, and even shocked. But I mustn't say any more. Not yet. And believe me, Dalice, I dread the time when I have to tell your father."

"He doesn't even know you went to school?"

"No. He decided to make that trip to Kokomo. To get it over with. There wasn't time for him to get back."

"One thing, Mom. Is there anything I can do? Is any of this my fault?"

"I've been asking myself the same questions, about my responsibility. And as for you I can't see how you can be blamed."

"Then I am in this. Or how Anitra feels about me."

Her mother nodded. "Yes. But she feels the same way about a lot of other people. That's what's affecting her work — or so the counselor feels."

Dalice looked down at her mother's folded hands. She clasped them so tight that her knuckles were white. "Mom. I'm sorry. I hate seeing you so upset. But maybe I can make things a little easier by telling you what you can't say. I know Anitra's jealous."

Her mother smiled through her tears, reached over and cupped Dalice's face in her hands, and nodded. "Now I must wash my face and get something on the stove. This deep thinking's giving me a headache."

Dalice said, "I'll be out to help in a minute." She sat at the table and tried to imagine how Anitra was feeling. *I'd be miserable if the school called Mother* in for a conference about me. I'd wonder if anyone I knew saw her go in the office. And I'd feel everyone was whispering that I was in some big trouble and trying to figure out what I'd done. I'd probably run home and hide.

She didn't want to go upstairs. She was sure Anitra wouldn't want to see her or talk to her. *But I have to change my clothes.* Then she remembered that she'd left a pair of blue jeans and a white cotton blouse in the carpenter shop.

She brushed a piece of paper to the floor as she rose from the chair. She stooped to pick it up and recognized the drawing her sister had started a few days before. *Poor little birds,* she thought. *Not finished yet. Your feathers are still ruffled and you are all straggly and hunched against the wind.*

Neither Dalice nor her mother mentioned the trouble as they prepared the evening meal. *It's like we're avoiding it to keep from feeling sad or crying,* Dalice thought. *I know this is going to be hard on my mother — trying to act as if everything's okay. Can she?*

"Is Grandma coming to eat? And how?" Dalice asked as she dropped frozen flowerets of cauliflower into boiling water.

"Oh, my goodness!" Eileen said. "I'm supposed to pick her up at the church at four-thirty." She looked at the clock. "There's still time. What am I thinking of — well, I guess we both know the answer to *that* question."

The telephone rang as Dalice turned the browning chops. She flicked the switch to "low" before going to the hall. "Is this Cornells?" a girl asked.

"Yes."

"The ones who used to live in Oakville?"

"Yes."

"Well, good. I'm Lou Evan Master."

"Oh, yes, I remember you. You were in Anitra's class. And lived across from the parsonage."

"Right. You're Enid Alice. I recognized your voice right away."

"Did you want to talk to Anitra?"

"Yes. You see, my mother brought me to Muncie after school. For a coat. We're in the mall. I saw the bookstore and thought of you. So I'm calling from a pay phone. That's why it's noisy sometimes."

"I'm sure Anitra will be glad. I'll get her. Hold on!"

Dalice had the feeling that this call from an Oakville friend might be part of what her sister needed. Lou Evan had been at the Cornells more than any other girl. She was a happy person who often said, "I'm not going to let mean things other people say bother me. That's their problem." The girls had cried when the Cornells decided to move. They vowed to visit each other often and call and write regularly. They kept in touch for about six months. Then they began to let go and their communications had been few and far between for over two years.

"Anitra," Dalice called. "You're wanted on the phone. Lou Evan Masters is calling from the mall." She heard her sister's feet thump on the bedside rug and clack across the hardwood.

Dalice turned to go back to the kitchen but she saw that Anitra's eyes were red and that her hair was tumbled.

66

The conversation lasted for nearly ten minutes. Dalice heard snatches of sound but no distinct words. She could tell that her sister's voice became more animated and she heard her laugh twice.

Eileen Cornell and her mother-in-law came in the back door while Anitra was talking. Dalice watched her mother's face and saw her eyebrows arch. "It's Lou Evan Masters from Oakville," she explained. "She's calling from the mall."

"Good," Eileen said. "She could always cheer Anitra."

"Does your sister need cheering?" Alice Cornell asked.

"A little," Dalice answered. "She's been sort of down lately."

"Well, that's normal with some people I guess — with all of us at times."

Dalice wanted to talk to her grandmother so much it frightened her. *Suppose I say things that worry her? Or that Mother'd rather I didn't mention?*

Anitra ran upstairs as soon as she said good-bye to Lou Evan. But she came down soon afterward, with her face scrubbed and her hair brushed into smooth waves, not curled into tight ringlets. She talked more at the table than she had the evening before, or for days. She asked her grandmother how many people were attending the convention. She asked her father if Kokomo store was larger than the Muncie branch of the chain. When Eileen Cornell started toward the refrigerator Anitra said, "I'll dip the ice cream, Mom."

She's making a special effort to be nice, Dalice thought. *Because she's in trouble? Does she think she can keep Mother from talking to Daddy? She should know better than that.*

"What time are you going back to church, Grandma?" Anitra asked.

"I'm not. Not tonight," Mrs. Cornell said. "The bishop's going to talk. I've heard him once. And to tell you the truth he's not that good a speaker. So if no one objects, I'll stay here."

"Who'd object?" Eileen said. "In fact we were wondering if we were going to see anything of you except to say 'hello' and 'good-bye.' "

"I've been thinking," Anitra said. "It's not fair for me not to share Grandma. You can sleep in the other bed, Dalice. I'll take the couch."

Dalice looked at her sister's face but couldn't read any meaning into either her tone of voice, or her expression. *Is all this niceness just a cover-up? Or what is it? Could she really be feeling sorry for the worry she's caused Mom?*

9

IT TURNED OUT that Dalice didn't have a bedtime talk with her grandmother that night. The whole
family played games and put a puzzle together for an
hour or so. Anitra asked, "Is it okay if I make buttered popcorn?"

"I have no objections," her mother said. "But I
for one am not hungry."

No. She wasn't at dinner either, Dalice thought. *She
hasn't had a chance to talk to Daddy yet. And probably feels all choked.*

"You'll eat some, won't you, Grandma?" Anitra
asked.

"A little. Just to be sociable."

"I think I'll go upstairs and do my homework," Dalice said. She had the feeling that if she broke away from the group the time for the talk between her parents would come sooner. *Besides I feel uneasy watching Anitra going all out to be nice.*

After she closed her books and put on her pajamas Dalice turned on her small FM radio. She wanted to be awake if her grandmother wasn't too tired to talk. She heard voices for a few minutes. Then no more sounds came from downstairs, or none that she heard until the next morning.

A brushing of fabric and the click of wire hangers woke her. She raised her head to see her sister backing away from the wardrobe. Anitra put a finger to her lips and then nodded her head backward. Dalice looked to the other bed. *Grandma's still asleep and it must be time to get up. Why is it so dark?*

She pulled her tan corduroy jumper and printed blouse from the closet and went to the bathroom. The door was locked. *Anitra will be in there, no telling how long. I'll scrub my face and hands downstairs and maybe have time to eat breakfast.*

She glanced out the south window of the living room and saw dark clouds overhead. Once she thought she heard a rumble. *Sometimes it does thunder in winter.* Her father looked up from the *Morning Star* and smiled. "Good morning, Dalice. Ready to start a new day?"

"I'd better be. It's here."

Eileen Cornell turned from the open refrigerator with a pitcher of orange juice in one hand and three eggs in the other. She bumped the door shut with her shoulder. Dalice thought she looked tired. Sha-

70

dows half-circled her eyes. "Anyone else up?" Eileen asked.

"Anitra. I think Grandma's still asleep."

"No wonder. We kept her up till almost midnight with our problems."

"You did? I didn't hear anyone talking."

"We went out to your room. Anitra was on the couch, " Eileen said.

David Cornell looked at his wife and wrinkled his forehead. "Dalice knows?"

"Just that I was called to school. No — she *knows* more than that, but I didn't *tell* her anything but the fact that I'd gone and a hint of the reason for the trouble."

Dalice wanted to ask a lot of questions but there wouldn't have been time for her parents to give the answers even if they were ready to talk. She couldn't help saying she was surprised that they'd mentioned the situation with her grandmother.

"We didn't bring up the subject," David Cornell said. "But she sensed something was wrong and said if it would help us to talk she had listening ears."

Dalice heard footsteps in the hall upstairs and had time for only one question. "Did it help?"

Her parents nodded. "You going to eat now, Dalice?" Eileen asked as Anitra came downstairs.

"I'll have time afterward. So I'll dress while the bathroom's not occupied." By the time Dalice went downstairs again Anitra had left for school and her grandmother was sitting at the table. "We're like ships that pass in the night, aren't we?" Mrs. Cornell said. "Our comings and goings don't coincide."

Dalice took time to drink a cup of hot chocolate and

71

eat a slice of cinnamon toast. "You're going to stay tonight, aren't you, Grandma?"

"Yes. The convention ends at noon. And your parents asked me to stay over. Then we'll all go to Oakville tomorrow after school — if that's agreeable to you girls."

"It's agreeable to me. In fact, it's great. And I think it will be to Anitra. She'd probably like to go see Lou Evan."

"Before you leave, Dalice," her father said, "your mother and I are to be at school at eleven. Anitra will be called in, and maybe things will get a new start."

"Does Anitra know?"

"Some. She's pretty uneasy about what may happen."

"Well," Dalice said. "I feel sorry for her. I can't help it."

"I know," her mother said. "So do I. But perhaps we have to go through this valley in order to get on top of the problem."

"A speaker at the convention said something about valleys yesterday," Mrs. Cornell said. "She told us there couldn't be a valley unless there were hills on either side. Then there's a higher place ahead, no matter which way you turn."

Nancy was not at the corner and Dalice didn't wait. The thunderclaps were closer and a few raindrops splattered on the walk. *It's so cold*! Dalice thought. *The rain must be close to freezing.*

Her school day proceeded as usual until she went to home ec class. The teacher said she was laying her lesson plan aside to talk about their home projects. "I want you to decide between now and Christmas vacation what project you're going to do. Then the actual work will begin at the start of the second semester."

Several girls groaned and five hands and several questions were raised. "What kind of project?" "What if we don't have any money?" "I'm not sure my mother will let me change anything around our house."

I don't have to decide what to do. My project is already started, Dalice thought. She was eager to tell Mrs. Kirtley about the plans for her room. She was surprised when the teacher said she'd be glad to talk to Dalice that afternoon if she'd get a pass from study hall. The bell for the next class rang and they were still talking.

"I'd suggest that you keep a notebook and take pictures, you know to show it before and after. Or make drawings. Your idea is so strong that it might have a chance in the state contest — if it's properly presented. Would that interest you?"

"I'm not much for competing, Mrs. Kirtley. But I would like to make the scrapbook whether I win anything on it or not."

"Are you afraid of failing, of not winning?"

"Well — I don't know. I don't think so," Dalice replied. "I was in the county spelling contest once and got mixed up on 'receive.' So I was second, which wasn't bad. Maybe it's not failing that bothers me, but the way things are spoiled when I get all worked up about beating someone."

Mrs. Kirtley smiled. "Perhaps you're wise — more so than people two or more times your age. But that is not so surprising. As a teacher I've seen many proofs that wisdom isn't age-bracketed."

Dalice thought about that conversation as she hurried up the ramp and down the hall to her last class. *I never realized this before. But the reason I don't like competition is that I get jealous feelings — like Anitra. Is she trying to compete with people — with me?*

Roll call was being taken in the last class when the principal made an announcement over the intercom. "School will be dismissed in five minutes. The temperature has dropped and the rain is freezing on walks and streets. Watch your step. Listen to the radio for announcements regarding school closings."

As soon as Dalice stepped out into the cold air thoughts of what had happened in the office at the junior high flooded her mind. They'd crept in all during the day, but she'd tried not to be overwhelmed by worry. She had a one-sentence prayer which was a key for locking fear out of her mind: "Let the goodness of God be felt now."

Nancy called, "Dalice, wait! We'll hold each other up." The concrete was already glazed. The girls walked across every path of grass they saw, their feet crunching the brittle iced blades. "It sure is beautiful," Nancy said as they waited at the corner for cars and buses to edge forward on spinning wheels.

"I guess," Dalice answered. "But I have to keep looking down and can't enjoy the scenery."

"Do you know what I'd like to do?" asked Nancy. "Take sleds to the lot behind the supermarket and slide down the bank. Willing?"

"Yes. If Mom agrees to it. Then maybe you could

come to our house for a while and meet my grand-mother."

"Oh! I didn't tell you! I did meet her. Her church and mine are in the same conference. Our choir sang last night. And she came up to me — because I had the solo. She found out I'm your friend. Didn't she tell you?"

"We didn't have much time to talk. And I can't keep still about this any longer, Nancy. Our family's not — well, we're upset. Anitra's having trouble at school. And this sort of clouds everything."

"Oh, I'm sorry," Nancy said. "If you'd rather not go sledding, I'll understand. It was just an impulse."

"Well, it *would* be better to wait and see how things are at home. There was a conference at school. I don't — well, I sort of dread to go home, for the first time in my life. I'll call you — either way."

Dalice turned down the alley and went through the back gate. The patches of grass were wider on this route. She took a deep breath as she turned the door-knob. The first thing she heard was the whirr of the sewing-machine motor. She peeked around the door of the Bee-Hive and saw her mother guiding a length of pink fabric under the dancing presser-foot.

Eileen must have sensed the presence of Dalice. She looked around and slid her half glasses farther down on her nose. "I didn't hear you come in. Did you slide home?"

"Not exactly. I tiptoed to keep from sliding and slipping. Where'd you get that material?"

"It's an old sheet. I had to be busy. So I fished a package of red dye out of the laundry cabinet, divided it, and came out with this color."

"It's perfect. Exactly like I pictured."

"Well, good! You don't have to use it permanently. But I thought it'd be better if you had curtains, since you're sleeping out there sometimes."

"Are you the only one here?"

"Yes. Your father picked his mother up at church. When he left school she wanted to shop in the mall and browse in the bookstore. I know what you're really asking, 'Where's Anitra and what happened?' "

Dalice nodded.

"She's probably on the way home. I hope!" Eileen said. "But it would be better if she told you about today. That's what Mrs. Hilton recommended. That Anitra do her own backtracking."

"Will she? It can't be easy."

"It certainly won't. But I think she realizes that she has to change her attitudes."

Dalice started toward her room and then she asked, "Is it all right if I go sledding over on the bank with Nancy?"

"If you're careful and don't stay long."

Dalice met Anitra coming through the kitchen. *She looks different, sort of subdued*, Dalice thought. On an impulse she said, "Want to go sledding with Nancy and me?"

"You want me?"

"Sure. Two can shove harder than one."

10

THE SLEDDING PARTY was over in a few minutes. The sled runners quickly cut through the ice coating. The girls had to take a new path on each downward swoop. "I guess this wasn't such a good idea," Nancy said. "Hard-packed snow makes better sliding. Want to go for a Coke?"

"Hot chocolate sounds better," Dalice said. "I've got enough money for two, Anitra. Or even three."

Anitra had talked on the way over even when no one asked questions of her. She was quiet on the way to Sally's Place. They were in sight of the electrically lighted strawberry cone when two girls came from the other direction. "I don't think I'll stop," Anitra suddenly said. "I have a bunch of homework. Here, I'll take the sled home." She took the sled and started toward their house. "See you," she called.

"What changed her mind?" Nancy asked. "I mean *does* she have to study?"

"Maybe. But I don't think that's the real reason she left. Those girls just ahead of us are in her class. One's Dana, who *was* Anitra's best friend. She's been avoiding her lately. Or it could be the other way around."

The air inside the store smelled of frying hamburgers, chocolate sauce, and assorted perfumes. Chattering voices and the soft music from an FM radio could be heard from the round tables and the three speakers. Dalice thought of something her father once said. "It's surprising that kids go to Sally's Place. No jukebox, no pounding rhythms, just music."

Dalice knew why it was the favorite meeting place of one segment of young people. The sandwiches were special. Most of the time the meat patties were larger than the buns. There were other advantages, like being able to hear and the fact that Sally enforced the "no smoking" rule. She said she didn't know how marijuana smelled, didn't intend to learn, and was taking no chances that it'd become anyone's habit in her place of business.

The girl with Dana tugged on Dalice's coat as she passed the table second from the front. "I saved a seat for Anitra."

"She went on home," Dalice said.

"But I saw her with you — coming this way."

"I told you she wouldn't come in. Not after she saw us," Dana said.

78

"What do you mean by that?" Dalice asked. But even as she spoke she wanted to turn and leave. *If Dana's going to say anything bad about Anitra I don't want to hear it.*

Wanting to avoid anything unpleasant was not new to Dalice. When she was younger she'd slip off and play alone if her friends quarreled or were angry at her. Later she began pulling away from the group if someone told a joke that wasn't funny to her, or was suggestive and shady. She was aware that this tendency set her apart. Tish Barnhart often taunted her by saying, "Well! If it isn't half of our goody-goody team." Dalice knew that Nancy was considered the other half.

Dalice had often wondered why it hurt at all to be ridiculed for doing what is right. *It should make me proud — like I'm on the right track — the one I chose to travel.* Other times she thought she was wishy-washy in not standing and defending herself openly. *But I can't here,* she thought. *Not with others around to hear what Dana may be thinking.*

Dalice walked home alone because Nancy had to go in the opposite direction and get some luncheon meat and snack foods from the market. "My brothers should bowl in the Young Sprout league this evening. But Mother's scared to drive on ice. So the Morrisons may eat at the same time for a change," Nancy explained.

A misty drizzle had begun to cloud the air and Dalice could tell that the ice coating was thicker than it had been when they stopped for hot chocolate. She walked slowly and a new thought came to her mind. *Does Dana have anything to do with whatever's hap-*

pened to Anitra? I don't really know her. When she comes to the house she wants Anitra to go upstairs or outside. And a lot of times she pulls her aside, cups Anitra's ear with one hand and whispers. I hate it when people do that. I'm always sure they wish I wasn't there.

The other Cornells were in the kitchen. Anitra was stirring something at the stove and the others were sitting at the table with their heads turned to the radio on the end of the table. Dalice stopped inside the door and listened. "Roads and streets in this area are already slick and hazardous," the announcer reported. "And this freezing rain will likely continue until midnight. Pedestrians as well as motorists are urged to stay at home."

"That does it," David Cornell said. "I'll be back in twenty minutes or so."

"But you heard the bulletin," Eileen said. "We're supposed to stay at home. You're not going to the mall."

"No. No. Wayne's closing up. And I doubt if there's much going on out there tonight. I'm just going across the alley. To borrow Jim's plane and electric sander."

Alice Cornell walked to the windows and pulled back the yellow-and-white-checked curtain. "Look," she said. "Nature has given you a glazed window. It's ice-covered. Well, you folks may have a boarder longer than you bargained for. This weather! We've had all varieties in this past week."

"Yes," Eileen said. "It's like people say about Indiana. If you don't like the weather, wait an hour or two."

David Cornell came back as vegetable soup was

80

being ladled into bowls. "It's really treacherous out there. I slid and slipped just going across the driveway! This is the kind of night when electric lines in the country could snap."

"That happens in Oakville."

"What do you do?" Dalice asked.

"Several things. First, when I see coatings of ice on twigs and wire fences I light the kindling and wood in the fireplace. Then I fill pans, kettles, and even the bathtub with water. The last move is to get out my box of candles. When there's no electricity, there's no heat and the water pump doesn't work."

"Sounds like fun to me. Like pioneer stories." Dalice exclaimed.

"It *is* cozy for a while," her grandmother said. "Then the inconveniences begin to show up, like being confined to the one warm room and the wavering of candle flames."

As he pushed his chair back from the table David Cornell announced, "It looks like the time schedule for working on the carpenter shop is going to be changed. I think I'll get at it."

"That's why you went to Jim's — for tools?" Eileen asked.

"That's why. Coming, Dalice? Or anyone? Or all of you?" David asked.

"It's my time to do dishes," Dalice said.

"Scoot on out," her grandmother told her. "I've been a lady of leisure long enough."

"What will you do first?" Dalice asked as she followed her father through the back porch.

"I've been itching to get at that carpenter's bench." He told her he hoped the plane and then the sander

81

would smooth the splintery places and take off the oil and paint stains. "I suppose it could be painted but a stain might make it blend with the walls. Which would you prefer?"

"The stain. Do they have it in shades of gray?"

"I think so. Or we could antique it. But first we'll try to uncover the natural grain."

"What can I do?" Dalice asked.

"I brought in a can of filler from the garage. You could fill the nail holes in the walls. Then when we use the wood finish they'll be hidden."

The steam hissed as it came in the radiator and the rain hit the window in muffled clicks. "Do you care if I bring a radio out here?" she asked.

"No. But if I have a choice I'd say the FM. I'd prefer soft music to alarming news or the top twenty." He turned and smiled as Dalice started toward the door. "Does my dislike of popular music bother you?"

"No," she said. "You have the right. Besides, a lot of it does sound alike. It gets a little boring sometimes."

As they worked against the background of soft music they talked about the next steps. David Cornell said the storage closet could be transformed into a wardrobe in a half a day and that he might have that time before the weekend if the ice storm continued. "There'll be little business tomorrow. Wayne lives across McGalliard and he can probably walk over."

Dalice was a little surprised to see Anitra when the back porch door opened. "I wouldn't like this. Coming through the cold, every time. It's shivery," she said.

"Well, it won't always be cold and besides Daddy's

Dalice sat on the bed and put her arms around her sister. "It's okay, Anitra. Do what you have to do when you can."

going to unboard that place over there — make the opening into the Bee-Hive."

"Yes, that's the last part of my share in this project. And I plan to finish it before another week rolls around."

I can get the wicker chair when we take Grandma home, Dalice thought. *And Mom has the curtains almost finished. The floor's okay as is — after we get it scrubbed. I can soon move in for sure. Maybe by Monday.*

"I sure hope this ice melts by tomorrow night," Anitra said. She was sitting cross-legged on the brass bed.

. . ."Why?" Dalice asked.

"Because, Mom said I could have Lou Evan in for a visit. I even got to call her long-distance a while ago."

"I'd think this ice will break sometime tomorrow," her father said. "It's not cold, barely below freezing. A little sun will bring about a lot of cracking and shattering."

"And I can sleep here," Dalice said. "No problem with that."

Anitra started to say something. All Dalice heard was, "I'm so — " She looked around and saw tears trickling down her sister's cheeks. She didn't ask what was wrong. Anitra was supposed to do the telling.

Dalice worked two pellets of wood putty into holes before Anitra spoke. "I'm — I have to tell you something, Dalice. At first everyone said I *had* to but now I'm beginning to want to say things. But not yet. It's too hard for me to put it all in words."

Dalice looked at her father. He cleared his throat

84

a couple of times, then turned away. Dalice sat down on the bed and put her arms around her sister, loving the feel of the curly hair and the lilac scent of Anitra's favorite cologne. "It's okay, Anitra. Do what you have to do when you can." She reached in her pocket and said, "Here's a Kleenex."

After Anitra left the shop Dalice drew a deep breath. "Being young's not always easy, is it?"

"Being any age is not *always* easy," her father said.

They worked for another hour, stopping only to drink cups of hot tea and eat crackers topped with pimento cheese spread. The surface of the workbench emerged, the burls and swirls of the grain standing out in a lovely design. "It's as I thought," David said. "This is one wide plank. A board like this would cost more than we could spend nowadays."

Dalice ran her hand over the smooth surface. "I've been thinking," she said. "I can do a lot of things here. Make a desk at one end and a bookshelf at the other and use the middle part for a dressing table."

"Wouldn't you want a mirror?"

"That's right. So I'll switch. Put the desk here. Then I can see out into the backyard." She glanced at the foot-wide space between the windows. "I need something to hang there. But it's got to be just right. I'll think about it."

11

EXCEPT to bring in the milk and look for the morning newspaper, no one left the Cornell house until four o'clock when the family drove to Oakville. The Bee-Hive was not the only area of unusual activity that day. A hammer thudded and a saw whined in the back room. Footsteps echoed on the stairs and the radio in the kitchen alternated news bulletins and music.

David Cornell finished his work on the storage cabinet before eleven o'clock. "The job wasn't as complicated as I thought it would be," he explained. He'd learned that the shelves weren't nailed to the sides, but rather rested on wall cleats and could be readily removed and rearranged.

Dalice scrubbed each rectangular section of wood and when it was dry she lined it with scented shelf paper. "I've had that for over a year," her mother told her. "You might as well use some before all the lemon fades away."

Dalice decided to move some things down from upstairs that morning — like her summer clothes and scarves she didn't wear often and the stacks of magazines she couldn't bear to throw away. Even as she worked, she wondered if Anitra would use this time at home to talk to her. *I wish she would and get it over with. It's no fun being uneasy around her. And I still don't know what kind of trouble she's in at school or how bad it is.*

Nancy phoned as Dalice was making one of her trips up the stairs. "You homebound too?"

"Yes," Dalice replied. "Isn't everyone?"

"Just about. Not a single car has gone down our street. Not even the paper boy made it. Two boys are trying to skate out front, but they're down more than they're up. I'm sort of enjoying myself. Kind of nice not going to school on Friday. What are you doing?"

"I'm moving," Dalice said. "Daddy didn't try to go to the store and he's getting a lot done in my room. It's looking great."

"Terrific! I want to see it. When I can walk without risking my neck or legs."

Anitra was more bubbly and less strained than she'd been for weeks. She worked at cleaning her room without being told and then stayed in the Bee-Hive for over an hour. Dalice stopped at the door once and asked, "What are you doing?"

"Oh, I'm trying to get these little birds to look right. Not so straggly."

Dalice paused for a minute or two then took a deep breath and went on out to her new room. *She's not ready to talk yet. And won't while Lou Evan's here.* She put the armload of magazines down on the kitchen table and went upstairs to find her mother or grandmother. She found both of them, each of them sitting on a twin bed sorting through boxes of scraps.

"Oh, there you are," Eileen said. "We called to you as you went through the hall. I guess you didn't hear us on account of the sweeper."

"What are *you* doing?"

"Hunting right colors to make your pillow tops. We want you to decide."

"Before I go home," Alice Cornell said, "I'll do the piecework. How would you like having the patches joined by feather-stitching?"

"I'd love it. But wouldn't that be harder?"

"No. Not harder. More time-consuming. But time I have."

Dalice picked several pink pieces, plain, and striped and checked with white. She decided they should be alternated with pearl gray studded with stars. "Before I go down I have to say something," she explained. "Anitra's not talked to me about whatever's going on. And I'm tired of worrying. What kind of trouble is she in anyway?"

Eileen looked at her mother-in-law who nodded and patted the bed. "Sit down, Dalice dear."

"I guess we haven't been fair," Eileen began. "We

88

have bent over backward in following the counselor's advice, not realizing how anxious you really are."

"I have been worried. I keep trying to figure things out."

Eileen explained that Anitra had been going downhill in her studies ever since the seventh grade. And she had really tobogganed this year. "It seems that she wouldn't work at anything if she didn't excel in it. As soon as someone topped her she lost interest."

"Was she like this at Oakville?" Dalice asked.

"Well, she often got first place there. You see this school is at least five times as large. There's more competition. It was easier to win at Oakville, and Anitra doesn't like being beaten. She's not used to it."

"Neither do I," Dalice said. "Not really."

"Yes, but there's a difference. Anitra wants to *be* best. Not work hard to be best."

"And I'm odd in another way," Dalice said. "I like working — at most things."

"Don't pin that label on yourself, Dalice," her grandmother said. "You're not as alone in that attitude as you may think."

"But I still don't understand — how has this affected Anitra at school, besides her grades?"

"She's resented those who moved ahead of her, becoming jealous and even hateful. If she heard of the success of anyone she turned on them. Mrs. Hilton says she doesn't get along well with people."

Dalice remembered the look on Dana's face when Janie Spencer asked about Anitra. *Is there a key there? Did Dana have anything to do with all of this?* she wondered.

89

"This feeling of jealousy is such a foolish waste," Mrs. Cornell said. "Grown-ups are guilty of it too. They think they become less when someone else accomplishes more."

Dalice looked at her grandmother and asked, "Will you repeat that last sentence?"

Instead, her grandmother put the same thought in different words. "The success of others doesn't diminish us unless we think it does."

"What you're saying is that no one can *make* anyone jealous, right?" Eileen looked at Alice.

"That's true, isn't it?"

"I guess so. But I'd never quite come face-to-face with that fact." She glanced at her watch. "Now I'd better face the fact that it's time to cook some lunch."

"Something easy, Eileen," Mrs. Cornell said. "Remember, I'm treating all of you at the new steak house on the way to Oakville."

"I'd better get busy, too," Dalice said. "I dumped a load on the kitchen table."

"Before you go," her grandmother began, "I want to tell you that I don't think you should worry about your sister. There's enough love in this family to overcome jealousy — and the agitation that feeds it."

"You think someone else has influenced Anitra?"

"I wouldn't be surprised — not one single bit."

The sun broke through the veil of clouds while the Cornells were eating lunch. Within an hour, water began to drip from the icicles that fringed the eaves of the house in shimmering crystal. Ice fell from twigs and fences in chunks and turned into a carpet of sparkling fragments. Traffic began to crawl and by three o'clock was back to its normal pace.

When the Cornells finally left Muncie, Dalice's room was ready for her to move in except for the opening into the Bee-Hive, rugs, and some other finishing touches. She'd found a long brass rod in the attic, her father had tacked brackets on the window facing, and together they had hung the pink curtains at the two windows. Dalice looked at it and chuckled. *Now, it's like I have a pink frame around the backyard.* The scrubbing of the floor was left to the end so that it could dry while they were away. Just before they left, Dalice came in and sniffed. *It smells so — clean — and woodsy.*

They saw the damage of the storm as they drove the eleven miles to the steak house. Twigs and small branches littered the roads and some large limbs had splintered off from trees under the weight of the ice. One telephone wire had snapped and the ends dangled from the poles. "Someone's not talking to anyone," Eileen remarked.

"That's what really makes me feel isolated at such times," Alice Cornell said. "As long as I hear a click when I lift a receiver I feel in touch."

The evening meal, a stop at the general store, and the trip to the attic took over two hours. "We never will get back to town," Anitra said. Lou Evan will think we're not coming for her."

"Never's a long time," commented David Cornell. "And how can Lou Evan doubt us? You've called her four times."

They stowed the high-backed wicker chair in the back of the station wagon.

"Give me three guesses about what Dalice will do

tomorrow," Alice Cornell said, "and I'll have two to spare."

"You're right, Grandma. Paint the chair."

"I always hate to drive away and leave her waving," Eileen Cornell said as they pulled away from the curb.

"But that's the way she wants things," answered David. "Besides, I feel close to Mom even if I'm not near. If that makes any sense."

"It makes good sense."

Dalice called Nancy as soon as she'd set the fan-backed chair in her room. "Could you come over and see how it looks? Not much like the carpenter shop now."

"It'll be about fifteen minutes. I'm right in the middle of rolling up my hair. See you."

Dalice hurried upstairs and dug a pair of old lamps out of a box in the closet. She'd put them away when Anitra coaxed the blue china one from their Grandma Cranor. *I always liked these better. And brass and linen go with the look downstairs.* She set a lamp on either side of the windows. *That's one thing we didn't have to do,* she noticed. *Mr. Jackson put outlets all along the bench.*

She turned on the lamp, flicked off the ceiling light, and sat down in the wicker chair. She liked what she saw and the vision of what was to be added made it even more pleasing. *There'll be patchwork pillows, at least two on the bed and one on the chair. And some kind of rugs on the floor. I'll have to think about that later. What I need is something on the walls, between the windows and over the bed.*

Someone rapped three times on the door. "Come in," Dalice said.

"Do you say that to everyone?"

"No one knocks like that except you, Nancy," explained Dalice, and laughed.

"But they could! I mean I don't have a patent or anything. Say, this place is — terrific! Even better than I'd imagined. Going to sleep out here tonight?"

"Yup!" Dalice said. "Lou Evan's here with Anitra but I would anyway. Tonight and from now on."

"What are you going to do tomorrow?" asked Nancy.

"I hadn't really thought. We've been so busy here. I guess we'll have to go back to routine. How about you?"

"I'm going with my family on a trip. Not to attend the bowling tournament. But it's in Evansville. My favorite cousin — and her family — live there. So I'll be with Phyllis. I'll be back Sunday."

After Nancy left, Dalice planned the next day. *I'll get up early and paint the chair. Then if Dad needs me I'll work at the store. Maybe I can earn money for rugs. Anitra will be busy entertaining Lou Evan. There's not a chance we'll have time to talk. So, I might as well not worry about that. Besides, it doesn't seem as important — or scary now. I understand more.*

12

WHEN DALICE opened her eyes the next morning she felt as if she'd been asleep for a week. She stretched her arms back over her head, closed her fingers around the two brass scrolls, and pushed down with her heels. *I don't remember a thing after Mom and Daddy came to the door to see if I was all right and to say good night.* She felt her wrist before recalling that she'd left her watch in the bathroom and was too sleepy to go back upstairs. *That's another thing I need — a clock.*

She sat up and looked out the windows. *Daylight's coming,* she noticed. *Some of the birds are flitting around in the trees. I can see all the way out to the back fence.*

She dressed in her oldest pair of jeans and a dark blue sweatshirt. She brought in several sections of newspapers and the paint and brush from the back porch. *I could work on the chair out here,* she thought, *but it's warmer in my room and it'll dry quicker there.*

She soon realized that her father knew what he was talking about when he said that working on wicker was tedious. She couldn't slap on paint with long strokes. She had to edge the bristles into the crisscross places. After the front of the fan back was painted she went around to the other side and saw places she'd missed.

Her father came to the door as she began to paint the arms. "You've been up a while," he said. "You had to — in order to get that much done. Want me to give your arm a rest?"

"Aren't you in a hurry to eat breakfast?"

"It isn't ready. Your mother's taking an extra snooze. How about you cooking something for me?"

"Okay," Dalice said. "But you don't have to do this. I mean I wouldn't want you to be late for work."

"I won't be. No deliveries got to town yesterday. So if I make it by nine I'll have an hour to catch up on things before the store opens."

Everyone in the house scattered in different directions that day and didn't come together until evening. Dalice finished putting on the first coat of wild rose pink before nine-thirty. She stepped back and looked at her work. Then she drew a deep breath. *It really needs a second coat,* she

95

sighed. *And I'd hoped one would do. But — I think it will be worth the work it takes to put on another. It's going to be absolutely beautiful — all pink and lacy.*

Her mother came to the bathroom door while Dalice was scrubbing the paint flecks from her face and arms. "I'm a splattery painter," explained Dalice, though it was so obvious that she hardly needed to have said it.

"So am I. I'd have polka-dot hair if I were in your place."

"What's on your mind?"

"Several things," Eileen said. "Mainly that I'm going uptown. Anitra and Lou Evan want to go shopping, the window variety mostly, and I need new boots. Mine leaked at the seams this week."

"What does Anitra want?"

She wouldn't tell me. Said it was to be a surprise and that she was using her own money."

"Her own — oh, she must mean what she earned helping Grandma Cranor rake leaves."

"What she earned, or what Mother gave her — anyway that's where the money came from. But what I meant to say is do you want to go?"

"Not to shop. But maybe I'll ride to the bus stop and go out to the mall. First, I'll call and see if they need help at the store."

Mrs. Norman answered the telephone. "Why are you working on Saturday?" Dalice asked. "You wanted the day off."

"I know. You see Wayne's been holding down the fort almost single-handedly and needs a break, and we're busy already."

96

"That's why I called. To see if Daddy wants me to help."

"My guess is that he does. I think people have been shut up as long as they can stand it. And the Christmas rush has definitely started. Excuse me for a second." Dalice heard muffled voices and the jangle of the cash register before Mrs. Norman said, "You're needed, young lady."

Dalice had mixed feelings as she went to her room to change her clothes. She knew she'd have enjoyed staying at home alone, either to curl up on the bed and read, or sit at her bench desk and study. *I'd like it even better if the chair were dry. It will be tomorrow and I can postpone the second coat for a day or two. Besides, I need another pint of pink paint.*

She worked at the store until three o'clock, taking out enough time for a quick lunch and a short saunter through two department stores. She stopped at the houseware sections and looked at wall plaques and pictures, but didn't buy anything. Nothing seemed right. *I'll have to think a while longer before I know what I do want.*

"You must learn a lot about people," Dalice said to Mrs. Norman during a brief lull in business.

"A lot of bad? Or good?"

"Both, I guess. But right now the bad's in my mind."

"I know what you mean. That last customer was a little unreasonable."

"A *little!*" Dalice exclaimed. "He was nasty — just because we didn't have a book that's out of print."

"Too often it's the other way, though. People hear about a book on radio or television and want to buy it before the publishers release it." Mrs. Norman stopped to add the prices of three paperbacks. "But there are touching incidents."

"Like what?"

"People often come to the desk — if no one's near enough to hear. They tell me they've either lost a loved one, or been divorced, or retired from lifelong jobs. They want to know if I can help them find a book to get them over their bad time."

"And you do?" Dalice asked.

"Well, I try."

Almost two hours passed before Dalice boarded the bus to Locust Street. The aroma of vanilla met her as she walked in their house. She heard the soft bang of the oven door and reached the kitchen as her mother was turning a layer of cake onto the folds of a white towel. "That for tonight?"

"No. But there's a sampler. Your Grandmother Cranor called. I invited her and Father in to eat with us tomorrow. She'd heard that we had other company from Oakville. The way she put it was, 'It does seem that you'd have some time for *your* family, Eileen.' "

"And she doesn't mean us — Anitra and Daddy and me?"

"No. But I can't go into that now. If I did I'd get all worked up and not be able to be civil tomorrow."

"Can I help?" Dalice asked.

"Yes, you can. The call from Mother came after I did the grocery shopping. Father likes caramel icing and I'm out of brown sugar. Would you go to the market?"

"Sure. Anything else?"

"You might get some snacks of some kind. For tonight. Here's some money."

Dalice's path crossed that of Scout Carson as she came to the entrance. He was carrying two brown sacks through the "out" door as the other swung inward for her. He nodded as she waved, and his chin ducked into the green leaves of a stalk of celery. She didn't take a wire cart to the aisles. *I can get around quicker*, she reasoned, *and won't have that much to carry.*

She looked for Scout at each check-out counter and stood in line at the one where he was sacking purchases. She'd seen him more often lately, both accidentally and on purpose. Sometimes she looked for him in the cafeteria and took her tray to the same table. He, just as often, brought books to the spot in the library where she'd gone to study. Dalice had thought a few times, *The home ec teacher'd probably say we're growing into a relationship. The way it seems to me, I already know who will be my first real date.*

"What you been up to?" Scout asked as Dalice set her selections on the moving counter.

"Working," Dalice answered. "I've been fixing up a room — for my own. And I helped out at the store today."

"That's good." Scout grinned. "Keeps you out of trouble."

Dalice smiled and took the sack from him. Neither could pretend she needed help to carry one pound of brown sugar, twelve ounces of cheese chips, and half that amount of corn curls.

The first part of evening after dinner was a quiet time for Dalice. She felt a little lonely because Nancy couldn't be expected to call or come over. *But there are other people and other things to do,* she told herself. She studied in her room until her father came out with a hammer and a heavy iron bar with a forked end.

"I'm ready to connect you with the rest of the house," he said. "Would you get that sheet of plastic from the back porch and spread it on the floor? There'll be some sawdust and splinters flying around here in a minute or two."

"You don't have to do this tonight."

"It won't take as long as you think. I'll probably get the new door up before bedtime. Then you'll have another job of painting. Say that chair looks good. Think it needs another coat?"

"Well, I've decided it would help. And I bought another pint today."

Dalice gathered up boards and carried them to the back porch as her father pried them away from the old door frame. "See," he said. "It's not such a big job." The louvered door was in place by ten.

Dalice could faintly hear sounds through the slatted slits but they were muted. "It *will* be better," she said. "I won't feel so alone out here."

"And your mother's mind will be more at rest."

Anitra and Lou Evan were curled up at either end of the couch with a bowl of snacks between them when Dalice went to the living room. They sat and talked a while.

After a while Anitra yawned and rubbed the back of her neck with the knuckles of one hand. "I guess I am sleepy."

"Before we go up," Lou Evan said. "I'd like to see your room, Dalice. Anitra told me about it. And I heard the pounding."

"Come on back," Dalice invited her. "I'll give you a personally conducted tour. I suppose you know it was once a carpenter shop. I imagine we'll call it that for a long time."

"I can imagine," replied Lou Evan. "We do that, too. My mother bought a dish cupboard years and years ago. It was green when it was new, but has been painted twice, first white then yellow. But we still put our cups and plates in the 'green cupboard.'"

"There are several things to do yet," Dalice explained to Lou Evan. "Like getting rugs. My grandmother's making patchwork pillow tops. And I need *something* on the walls. Like between the window and over there."

"I think this is a real neat place," Lou Evan said. "Ready to go, Anitra?"

Dalice turned around in time to see what her sister was doing. She was leaning over the carpenter's bench and seemed to be measuring the space between the window with her hands. *Why?* she asked herself. *What is she thinking?*

13

"*MY NOSE would have told me this room was open to the rest of the house,* Dalice thought before she opened her eyes the next morning. The aroma of coffee and other cooking foods came through the louvered section of the door. *I'd better get up, to see if I can help, and still have time to get ready for Sunday school.*

She wrinkled her nose as she stopped at the kitchen doorway. "What all is cooking? I can't sort out anything, except coffee."

"A chicken's stewing for one thing," her mother explained. "My frozen noodles will come in handy today. And I'm stirring egg mayonnaise. You smell the vinegar. Mother turns up her nose at ready-prepared."

"You're not going to church?"

"Yes. That's why I'm doing all this bustling around keeping three or four pots bubbling. Besides, Mother won't miss out in Oakville. She's afraid something will go on she doesn't approve of."

"Mom! that's two critical remarks you've made about Grandmother Cranor in two days. You're not usually so — "

"Picky," Eileen interrupted. "I know. And I'm not exactly proud of myself. But things have come to the surface in the past few days. No. That's not the way it is. The truth's been here for me to see. I just didn't focus."

"All of this has to do with Anitra's trouble."

Eileen nodded as she sifted salt into the pot of bubbling chicken broth. "By the way, has she talked to you yet about her feelings?"

"No, but she came close. Mom, I felt so sorry for her. She cried."

"I know. Your father told me that. I've been thinking about a phrase from the Bible, something about a broken and contrite heart. It seems sad that we don't learn about our mistakes until we're hurt by them. Sometimes that's the only way."

"Is there anything I can do to help you?" Dalice asked.

"Yes. Get Lou Evan and Anitra up — so we all can have breakfast at once. Afterward, you can put extra boards in the table and set it while the girls and I do dishes."

Eileen's managing mind got everyone to church on time, even five minutes before the opening hymn.

Dalice enjoyed the Sunday school lessons but had never felt she was part of the class. Most of the girls had always attended Gethsemane Church, moving up together from the cradle department. No one had been unfriendly and she'd never been excluded from the class activities. *Even so,* Dalice often thought, *most of the time they talk about things which happened before I moved here. I feel on the fringe of things.*

She met her mother on the stairs as everyone moved to the sanctuary. "There's to be a short business meeting. To hear the report of the committee on Sunday school literature. So the worship service will be short. I'm going to slip out. Tell your father, will you?"

Dalice usually sat with other young people during the service. Instead, she slipped in at the end of a pew beside her father. He smiled and scooted over, his tweed suit making faint squeaking sounds on the varnished wood. They didn't speak after Dalice whispered the message. Part of the time she paid full attention to what the minister was saying. Now and then her mind wandered. She watched the sun lighten the pieces of stained glass of the windows on the east side. The beams of light made dull red into shimmering ruby and flat purple into shining amethyst. Those on the west did not have the same glow.

They usually drove to church in the winter, but the sun was so warm and the sidewalks so clear and dry that they decided to walk. They stopped and talked to friends or called to them from across the street. "Dana would say we're acting like country bumpkins," Anitra said.

"The country badge, I wear proudly," David Cornell replied. "The bumpkin tag, I resent. There are inept and awkward people everywhere."

"I wonder," Dalice asked. "Why do people like Dana say such things?"

"Probably because they've heard someone else say it. And they don't stop to realize country people live in wider more open spaces. They have to call to others in louder voices."

The girls had changed their clothes and had been downstairs for over a half an hour before Dalice heard steps on the front porch. She was closest to the door and had it open before her Grandpa Cranor had taken off his boots. "Why the boots?" she asked. "There's no snow."

"That's what I told him," Enid Cranor said.

"You never can tell. You never can tell. It pays to be prepared."

Anitra came from the kitchen and her grandmother said, "There's my girl. I was afraid you were sick when you didn't come to meet me."

Anitra glanced toward Dalice. "I'm fine, Grandma. Did you know Lou Evan is here?"

"Yes. Your mother mentioned it. So I called and offered to take her back to Oakville. To save her parents a trip."

Enid Cranor didn't offer to help finish up dinner. She never did. She wandered around looking at the table, picking up candlesticks from the windowsill, or running a finger around the base of the brass desk

105

lamp. Sometimes she sat for a few minutes on the edge of the ladder-backed chair and listened — or so it seemed — to what the men were saying. When she wandered to the kitchen she stood far away from the stove.

"That's a lovely dress, Mother," Eileen said. "It must be new."

Mrs. Cranor smoothed the folds of the lavendar silk and straightened the wide white embroidered cuff. "Yes, I bought it Friday. We went to Indianapolis to the mall after I saw that new doctor."

"Friday," Eileen repeated. "That's the day we were in Oakville. That's why I didn't get an answer when I called."

"Well, I heard you were there. And that Alice was *here* all that time. She made it a point to get me told that she had a nice long visit with *her* family. She'd never miss a chance to needle me."

Eileen was holding the portable electric mixer in her hand and had reached toward the wall plug. She put the appliance on the table with a thud. Dalice looked at her and saw glints in her gray-green eyes. "Mother," Eileen said. "Your tone of voice and insinuations infuriate me. Mother Cornell calls you because she thinks you want to hear news of us. It's that simple. And I'm going to say something that's been jelling in my mind for a long time: it's your jealousy that tinges your interpretations of her words and sharpens yours."

Dalice was spooning pineapple whip into sherbet dishes. She glanced at her grandmother and saw that her lips were pursed tightly. *Is she hurt or angry? Or both?*

The kitchen was quiet for two or three minutes except for the clack of the wooden spoon on the sides of the yellow bowl and the bubbling of noodles in the deep enamel pan.

"I can't quite believe that you've said what I just heard," Mrs. Cranor managed to say. Her voice was high and strained.

"Well, I did," Eileen said. "And I don't intend to argue with you or even bring up the subject again. But Mother, your jealousy is not only hard on others — it must be harmful to you."

"Why should I be envious of Alice Cornell? What does she have that I don't enjoy?"

"As I said, Mother, I'm not going to argue. Now can we act civil and not let this — this encounter — spoil the day for the others?"

Enid Cranor said very little during the mealtime, yet no one but her daughter and Dalice seemed to notice the silence. As the cake was being served, Joe Cranor asked, "How are things at the store, Dave? Do they work you hard weekends, or is the boss a privileged character?"

"I'm not the boss in the usual sense of the word. Just a manager. And I work extra many weekends. Usually the part-time college students we hire are eager to get in a few more hours. They have more time on weekends."

"I sort of figured on seeing the store," Mr. Cranor said. "For more than one reason. Surprising as it is, I've taken up reading since I retired."

"Then we'll go over to the mall," David said. "Everyone willing?"

They started to stand up and go to the closet

for their coats. At first Enid Cranor hesitated. Then she glanced at Eileen and suggested, "I could go window shopping for a mesh purse to carry when I wear my long velvet skirt."

"Did you kids know Mama had a long tail now?" Joe asked.

"Don't be vulgar," Enid said as she buttoned the small mink collar of her coat.

Dalice had the feeling that her grandmother was going just to avoid having a private conversation. *She's not in the mood to hear anything else Mom says, not even to talk to her.*

It was four o'clock before they recrossed town. Grandma Cranor was a little more relaxed on the way home. "I spotted a gold mesh purse I'm going to buy the next time I'm shopping at the mall," she said.

"Did you get your books, Grandpa?" Anitra asked. "Is that what's in that bag?"

"Your father gave me some damaged paperbacks," Grandpa said. "I had no idea so many good books are put out in paperback. I can afford to build me up a library now."

"But they don't look as nice on shelves," his wife said.

"Don't worry, Mama. I'll keep them in my escape hatch. Out of sight of your fine-feathered friends."

"I didn't know about that place — your escape hatch," Dalice said.

Her grandfather pulled her aside as they walked toward the car. "This is a sore subject with your grandma, because of the expense. I fixed up some of the room above the garage. Even bought paneling and a couch. Everything else is old — but comfortable."

"Say!" Dalice said. "You don't know about my new room, do you?" She only had time to tell him where it was before they reached the car. "I'll show you when we get back," she whispered.

She asked herself why she hadn't spoken aloud. *Everyone else knows but Grandma. Don't I want her to see how the carpenter shop has changed? Or do I think she wouldn't approve or even be interested?*

Joe Cranor made Dalice feel good with his approval. "You could grow up to be one of those high-priced interior decorators," he said.

"I don't know, Grandpa. Perhaps not many people would like barnsiding on their walls or a plank for their desk and dressing table. But it suits me fine."

"I've got something you might like. Now if you don't, just say so. But my mother had a small wooden clock, shaped like a house, stained gray, and it has a brass pendulum about the size of a silver dollar."

"Oh, Grandpa, it sounds perfect. I was going to buy a clock."

"Well, this one keeps good time. I kept repairing it even after Mama said it wasn't classy enough for her walls. I'll bring it in to you first chance I get."

Eileen was wrapping two wedges of cake in foil when they walked into the kitchen. "Here's a snack," she said as she kissed her father's ruddy cheek. "You certainly look well."

"I work at it," Joe Cranor said. "I don't read all the time. I didn't get this news in edgeways. I've been helping out with a vocational project over in Henry County. Supervising boys who are learning to

109

use tools. Resource person is what I'm called. Pretty high-toned label for me."

"Well, it's evidently good for you and I'm glad," Eileen said.

Lou Evan and Anitra came downstairs as the Cranors were walking toward the front door.

"I've had such a wonderful time, Mrs. Cornell — and Dalice — and Mr. Cornell. And I want Anitra to stay with me soon. Okay?"

"When it's all right with your mother," Eileen said. "You see," Anitra said. "That's not changed! We never could visit unless both mothers consented."

"It's nice that you girls are getting back together again. Loyal and true friendships are few and far between," Enid Cranor said. Then she turned to Anitra. "You haven't let me know, dear. Whatever happened about that art prize? Did they ever find out that the winner traced her drawing? Or apologize and make things right with you? Or do anything to that horrible girl?"

Dalice looked at her mother. *She looks as puzzled as I feel.* Then she glanced at her sister. Anitra's face was flushed even to her hairline. She was looking down at the floor. She seemed to sense that everyone was waiting to hear what she had to say.

"Well, it really wasn't exactly like I thought at first," Anitra said. "I mean the person who told me might have been mistaken."

14

DALICE had two telephone calls before she went to her room to do her homework. One came while the Cornells were having what Eileen called a pick-up supper. Each member of the family chose what they wanted to eat from the leftovers and the store of food in the refrigerator.

Nancy called first saying, "Well, we made it. Or did you know Evansville had an ice storm?"

"No. I haven't heard any weather news. Was it bad?"

"It was terrible. Two or three times my father wished we hadn't started back. But finally we drove out of it. So, I'm late getting at my homework."

"Mine's not all done either. We had company."

Both girls told about their weekends, and Nancy promised to come over Monday to see Dalice's room.

Dalice was washing the dishes and silverware she'd used when the second call came. She was surprised to hear Dana Forrest's voice. "Don't say anything — I mean not my name. I don't want Anitra to know that I'm calling?"

"Why not?"

"I mean — like I don't want her to think I'm prying into her business. Like, it might make things worse for her."

"What things?"

"Oh, you know what I mean. Like why she was called into the counsellor's office and everything."

Dalice stretched the cord so she could see into the living room. Anitra wasn't there.

"Are you there, Dalice?" Dana asked.

Her voice sounds — scared. Why is she afraid. But what business does she have calling anyway. "Yes, Dana. I'm still here. And you're absolutely right. This *is* Anitra's business — unless it's somehow yours also?"

"Well! I'm sorry I called!" The connection broke with a snap.

She is worried, Dalice thought as she went to her room. She ran her hand over the seat and back of the wicker chair. *Not bad,* she decided. *But it does need another coat.*

She'd finished outlining the chapter on the expansion of the United States to the West when Anitra came to the door. "Busy?" she asked.

"No. I just got the pioneers through the Cumberland Gap. Sit down. Try the chair."

"I'll take the bed. You know, Dalice, that's another reason I envy you. The way you study history. You make it sound as if you were there."

"That's because I like it, and probably because it's easy. Like art is for you. And math! You're a whiz in that compared to me."

"Maybe so," Anitra admitted. "But what I came in to talk about was — well. . . ." She started to cry. "Well, I came to talk about the envy thing. I guess I really mean jealousy. You know it's got me in trouble."

That it has, yes. But how and why I can't figure out. Why should you be jealous of me? You're much prettier and have lots of — "

"Friends. You were going to say I had lots of friends, weren't you? Well I don't, not now anyhow. I think they all left because I got so jealous."

"You do have friends. Back in Oakville and when we first moved here. When — "

"I can tell you when. Mrs. Hilton said this, and I think now maybe she was right. I let myself be changed when I began to run around with Dana."

Anitra went on talking for over fifteen minutes. She said that Dana had been the only girl to come up to her on the first day. Although other girls were friendly later, Dana had monopolized her as she was now doing Janie Spencer. At first Anitra had been flattered to be singled out by anyone like Dana. No one else was as striking in appearance. Dana's long black hair and dark eyes made her seem sophisticated and older than her years.

"After a while I saw that most kids didn't like her.

113

Not the ones who'd known her for a long time."

"Do you know why?" Dalice asked.

"Now I do. She causes trouble. She — well tells things that aren't quite true."

"Like saying the winner of the art prize traced?"

"Yes. And I believed her. Because I wanted to win. I'm not like you, Dalice. I like to be in the spotlight. And if anyone else is getting approval, I'm jealous. That's why it's made me mad to see you get attention."

"But you haven't always been that way."

"No. But lately — well, it seems if you don't do anything about bad feelings you have more of them."

"Yeah, I suppose so. That's sort of how I feel," Dalice said.

"Don't give *me* any credit for it. Daddy pointed it out to me. But do you know something! I noticed for the first time today how Grandma Cranor favors me. Why weren't you jealous?"

Dalice smiled and shrugged one shoulder. "Probably because I feel loved as it is. And I don't know quite how to say this, but having someone approve of you or of anyone doesn't make me feel — well, left out or unworthy. That's the only way I can say it."

Anitra said that she'd not taken art because of the way she felt about not winning the year-end award for excellence. She realized that she'd cheated herself because school was dull when she wasn't working at her favorite subject.

"I see all of this — and at least understand myself a little better. But it's going to be hard to change. Most of the girls probably think I'm like Dana. They

"I noticed for the first time today how Grandma Cranor favors me," Anitra said. "Why weren't you jealous?"

probably don't want to have anything to do with me. And I can't really blame them."

"What will you do about Dana?" Dalice asked.

"That's no problem. She's putting her noose around Janie Spencer's neck now."

"I doubt if that's happened yet." Dalice told her that Janie had saved a place for Anitra in the drugstore. I think she really wanted you to sit with her. "Why don't you call her? Show that you're willing to be friendly."

"I might. You know, having Lou Evan here made me feel a lot better. Not so — not like a total outcast."

Then Anitra curled up on the bed and clasped one of the pillows in her arms. "Glory be! My brain's tired. I'm not used to all this serious talk. What could we do for fun?"

"I heard that," said Eileen Cornell as she walked in. "What do you have in mind?"

"Any suggestions?" Dalice asked.

"As a matter of fact, yes. Dad wants to go for a walk. He says it's not too cold out."

"Oh, I bet it is cold," Anitra said smiling. "But if we walk briskly enough to keep warm, I'm willing."

The four Cornells went as far as the university. They circled the drive behind the administration building and passed the library and arts buildings. They met a few students and others passed them. "Think you'll go to school here someday?" Anitra asked.

"Probably," Dalice said. "But I'm not sure what I'd take. I change a lot. Whenever I take something new I get all excited and think I'll change my goal. But one thing I won't major in is math."

116

"I know what it would be for me already," Anitra said.

"Art."

"Yup! I could work on a drawing or painting or even in modeling clay and I could take all the time I wanted. Which makes me think of something I want to do tonight. I hope we head home soon."

"What — or should I ask?"

"You can ask — but I won't tell you."

"There's a special I want to watch," Eileen Cornell said as they crossed the backyard. Anyone object if I choose the channel?"

"Not I," Dalice said. "I'll watch with you."

"And I have some invoices to check," David Cornell said.

"How about you, Anitra?" Eileen asked.

"I'm going to the Bee-Hive too. I'll be quiet, Daddy. But first I want to use the telephone."

Dalice went to her room for her pink robe and woolly slippers. But before she got out of hearing distance she heard Anitra say, "Information? I'd like the number of the Spencer family in Brewington Woods. They're new."

Anitra was still talking when Dalice went to the living room and became engrossed in the story. During one station break Eileen asked, "Did you and your sister have a good talk?"

"Really good," Dalice said. "She's learned a lot."

"Well, I think the time is coming when all four of us can talk about this for once. Then we can go from there."

Anitra was still at the card table when Dalice went through the Bee-Hive to her room. "Look the other way," her sister said, crossing arms over her work.

"That might be dangerous. I could run into something."

"Walk straight and you'll make it. Even if you do look sideways."

Dalice walked into her room and turned the knob of her FM radio to soft music. She decided to read until she felt sleepy.

She heard footsteps and looked up to see her father. She'd expected Anitra, but she had evidently gone to the living room.

"I've been thinking," David Cornell said.

"Which is not unusual! About what in particular?"

"About Anitra — and you, and the fact that you work part time — have a chance to earn money."

"You mean it's not fair to her. I've had the same feeling."

"I've thought of a way to even things out — if she's willing. How would it be if she took over some of the jobs on your work chart?"

"And I pay her something?"

"That's what I had in mind. Of course, you'd have less money."

"But it *would* be fair. And somehow I think Anitra will like the idea. Will you bring it up?"

"Shouldn't you?"

"Yes. That probably would be better."

Dalice read for half an hour more, then listened for sounds from the Bee-Hive. Paper rustled once in a while and she could hear the clack of a pencil on the tabletop. Anitra was back at work.

A little while later Anitra came to the door with

her hands behind her back. "I'm ready to unveil my great surprise. But suddenly I'm not so sure you'll like it. And if you don't I won't be hurt. I mean, we all don't like the same things. That's perfectly natural. After all — "

Dalice smiled as her sister talked and held out her hand. "How can I know whether I like whatever it is if you don't quit talking and let me see."

Anitra became serious, so intent that Dalice wondered if she might cry. "I have to say this on behalf of me. I had you in mind when I started working on this again. Even before I was ready to admit I was jealous. I'd have given it to you even if we hadn't sort of made up. Or can people really make up if only one is mad? Anyway, I do want you to have it."

"I believe you," Dalice assured her.

Anitra walked toward the wild rose chair and gave Dalice a framed picture. She saw the back first and read the words, "To My Sister, Dec. 3, 1975."

Tears came to Dalice's eyes as she turned the burnished brass frame and saw the drawing: two gray birds huddled on a spray of bare, black branches. Their feathers were not ragged or straggly, but just ruffled into a lovely pattern.

"Oh, Anitra — nothing could please me more, nothing could be as right for between my windows."

"That's what I thought," Anitra said. "I've even put a nail in the wall. Daddy helped me space it — while you were working Saturday."

"Saturday," Dalice said. "That's when a lot of things still seemed mixed up. And all the time you were working on this. Good *was* going on."

"Isn't it always?" Anitra said.

119

DOROTHY HAMILTON was born in Delaware County, Indiana, where she still lives. She received her elementary and secondary education in the schools of Cowan and Muncie, Indiana. She attended Ball State University, Muncie.

Mrs. Hamilton grew up in the Methodist Church and participated in numerous school, community, and church activities until the youngest of her seven children was married.

Then she felt led to become a private tutor. This service has become a mission of love. Several hundred girls and boys have come to Mrs. Hamilton for gentle encouragement, for renewal of self-esteem, and to learn to work.

The experiences of motherhood and tutoring have inspired Mrs. Hamilton in much of her writing.

Mrs. Hamilton is author of four books of adult fiction: *Settled Furrows* and a trilogy on family relationships, *The Killdeer*, *The Quail*, and *The Eagle*.

Her books for children include: *Anita's Choice* (Mexican-American farm labor), *The Blue Caboose* (housing for the poor), *Busboys at Big Bend* (Mexican-American friendship), *The Castle* (rich girl, poor girl), *Charco* (inner-city boy), *Christmas for Holly* (foster child), *Cricket* (owning a pony), *Jason* (trade school vs. college), *Jim Musco* (a Delaware Indian), *Kerry* (growing up), *Linda's Rain Tree* (black girl changes schools), *Mindy* (her parents divorce), *Neva's Patchwork Pillow* (Appalachia girl), *Straight Mark* (countering drugs in junior high school), *Tony Savala* (a Basque boy), *Winter Girl* (jealous sisters), and *Rosalie* (Midwest farm life 50 years ago).